M.A. MOLLENKOPF

# The Fantasy Casino Murders

*A Detective Jack Stewart Mystery*

ISBN (paperback): 979-8-9887692-6-2
ISBN (hardcover): 979-8-9887692-8-6

Editing by David Yurkovich
Editing by Jason Letts

This book was professionally typeset on Reedsy.
Find out more at reedsy.com

*To my mother, Jacqueline ("Jackie"). Your inherent toughness and unwavering grit have served as the bedrock for Jack Stewart's character – a reflection of the strength and resilience you instilled in all your children. Thank you for believing in me, for the countless invaluable life lessons, and for always being my greatest champion. I love you.*

# Contents

# Preface

Writing this book has been a journey. Jack Stewart began as a man seeking justice in a world of shadows. Yet, the more I wrote, the more he revealed a darker truth, a stark departure from the man he once was. He wrestles with a darkness within, a volatile nature he struggles to keep in check. Jack's struggle echoes the legend of Jekyll and Hyde, a constant battle to contain the violent force that threatens to erupt, a force that could harm the very people he's sworn to protect. As he investigates a series of escalating crimes centered around the glittering Fantasy Casino, Jack finds an unexpected lifeline in Sarah, a brilliant and acutely perceptive computer forensics analyst. Their unlikely partnership, a seasoned detective and a nineteen-year-old prodigy, becomes a testament to the enduring power of human connection, a fragile hope against a descent into darkness. This is a story of a man fighting to control the monster within, a gritty mystery interwoven with threads of profound relationship evolution.

# Acknowledgments

I extend my deepest gratitude to the team who helped bring this book to life. First, I am profoundly thankful to David Yurkovich, who has served as my core editor and mentor for the past three years. His expertise extends far beyond impeccable grammar and adherence to the Chicago Manual of Style. He has been instrumental in helping me learn the art of storytelling itself. I owe David a debt of gratitude that words can scarcely express. Second, to Jason Letts, whose skills and guidance as an editor have been invaluable in shaping Jack Stewart from his earliest conceptions in both books. His keen eye and insightful feedback have been instrumental in crafting the narrative you now hold.

# Chapter 1

I knew someone was going to die today. I just didn't know how sad and devastating it was going to be.

The picture of Ginger felt like a curse: her dark brown hair, emerald eyes, and that ridiculously enticing smile. It always brought a fleeting hope, even now, six weeks after she stopped answering my calls. Her image fractured and pixelated as a text message notification, blazed across my phone's tiny screen. My eyes narrowed, "Come to room 114, unarmed in five minutes or your cop friend here is going to get nailed to the floor." My mind raced down dark paths as I handed my cell phone to Chief Borland, the chief of police for Wellspoint, Ohio. His stone-faced jaw clenched as he read the text message on the phone, then raised his eyes to meet mine while handing the phone to the special agent.

"I'm going in. We can't risk Schultzy's life on this operation going the way it was planned," I said as I removed my trusty Glock pistol from its waist holster and handed it toward Chief Borland.

The lights from the hive of computer screens reflected dimly off Special Agent Jenkin's face as he read the message. He dropped his head an inch or two in thought, then focused on Chief Borland and me. "You can't go in, Jack. It will screw up months of planning. We are taking him down tonight when our contact tips us. That's the plan, and we are not deviating from it. We won't catch him alone again for months."

Chief Borland didn't look at the agent; hell, he didn't even acknowledge his comment. He kept looking at me with those deep creases in his forehead as if he was trying to read my freaking mind. At fifty-eight, his once dark black hair had surrendered to a distinguished silver pewter, but it didn't reduce the determination in his eyes. Finally, he shifted just an inch in his half-height chair and said, "Okay, Jack, go get Schultzy, you need to play this very cool. He holds all the cards. For now."

"You are not in charge of this operation, and he's not going anywhere. We've worked far too long to let this butcher escape just because one of your officers screwed up and got caught."

Rain pounded the mobile police headquarters' roof, making it hard to concentrate as Chief Borland twisted his body a few degrees to face the special agent. "Agent Jenkins, your plan no longer fits the situation. I'm sending him in to fetch my deputy. I know it's risky, but I trust Jack can de-escalate, get this situation under control, and get my man out."

"Borland, if you do this, I'm going to ensure you pay the price for the cost of this operation and—"

Chief's voice rose sharply as spittle flew across the space between them, saying, "That's my officer being held hostage in there, Jenkins, and I'm starting to get the sense there's a lot you aren't telling us about the bigger picture, starting with how they knew Sergeant Schultz was a cop."

Another message popped into my phone. "You got three minutes, then I'm starting in on your boy here."

Agent Jenkins's temple veins bulged as he read the message and handed the phone back to Chief Borland, who then pitched it to me.

"Jack, listen to me carefully. Do not look for a way to take this guy on. Get Schultzy and get back here, no matter what you see in there or what he says. Do you read me? Schultzy is the op."

"Got it," I replied as I started working through courses of action in my head to extract Schultzy, then nail the bastard. I shuffled out the back of the vehicle, considering how to seize opportunities in the hotel, leverage everyday objects as weapons if needed, and try to outthink that dirtbag.

I pushed down the thoughts of Schultzy's wife and infant son as I kept telling myself to stay under control and fight back the brewing anger that's gotten me into so much trouble over the years. I fast walked through the dark, pouring rain across two parking lots and slowed down to enter the hotel's front door. The rain felt like icicles slicing down my back as I tried to get my head prepared for what I might encounter inside. I thought about the action Schultzy and I saw together in the war and how many times he bailed me out. Despite his diminutive size, he was a fantastic soldier.

I entered the brightly lit, under-construction lobby with purpose in my stride. I scanned the room and spotted a man with a gun in his left hand leaning on the concierge counter, where a very nervous young female hotel employee was standing. I felt vulnerable without some kind of weapon. The guy was well-dressed, skinny, solid chin, probably thirty years old, and about six feet tall with thick dark hair styled just so on his head. He looked surprisingly well-groomed for a criminal.

"Cutting it close, cop. I was hoping the boss would let me tune your partner up at least a little. Put your hands up and turn around. I gotta frisk you."

As he approached, I noted a scorpion tattoo on his neck. Then I raised my hands and turned slowly to get a good look around the lobby, hoping to get eyes on any other bad guys or civilians. I didn't see any.

"So what do I call you? Lex Luthor?"

"Luthor? No, Cop, you can call me Russ, just like everyone else."

His speech was punctuated by an unexpected 'th' sound where an 's' should have been, a lisp that made him hard to understand.

"Okay, you're clean. You feel this, Cop?"

I considered making a move on him just as I felt the cold, round muzzle of what was probably an old-fashioned revolver pushed into the base of my neck. "Yeah."

"Good, It's my Smith and Wesson. You are a big boy, so don't push me. It's going to be right here this whole time, so if you get cute, I'm going to finish you off nice and quick. Don't worry, it will sever your spine painlessly, and don't hate; it's just business. Now, let's go down the hall to room 114. You first."

He nudged me forward, so I slowly lowered my hands and started walking down the hotel's main hall toward room 114. I didn't see anyone else in the hotel lobby area, so that was good.

"Knock on the door."

I knocked on the door, and a very large man holding an industrial-strength-looking nail gun opened it. He was at least six feet, six inches tall with sparse brown hair and a black and red scorpion tattoo on the left side of his neck. His sapphire-blue eyes lit up when he saw me.

"Well, you made it. Good for you. Actually, good for him," he said as he turned his head, looking at a row of three chairs placed against the wall with a person zip-tied to each one of them and a bag over each of their heads. Russ nudged me forward, and I took two big steps into the large suite before the big guy said, "That's far enough."

I quickly scanned the room. I could see computer screens that were just out of clear view with two likely criminals working on them.

I wasn't expecting two additional hostages, two more bad guys pointing guns my way, two computer bad guys, plus Russell Spake. *These guys knew we were coming*, I told myself.

"I know you have this place staked out, and I'm gonna tell you what's going to happen," he started with a deep raspy voice of a chain smoker. "One, we are going to do some introductions, and then, two, I'm going to show you how deadly serious I am. And then, I might let you leave with this cop if you say the right things. Three, you are going to call off the dogs out there and leave by the top of the hour. Then we are going to leave. That's what's going to happen. If you piss me off, I'm going to fucking kill all of you right here, right now. Do you understand, *cop?*"

"Yes," I said, calmly and evenly as the muzzle of Russ's pistol dug into my back. This guy seemed really wound up, angry, and yet focused all at once.

"Good. Now I know from his phone that your name is Jack. I also know that you two have a relationship, and he's even shared pictures of his son. So, just to complete the circle, my name is Dimitri, and I work for very powerful people who want you cops to get out of our way or else some serious family issues could crop up. Do you understand? I wouldn't want this cop's baby to end up in an oven or something. You wouldn't want that, would you, Jack?"

"No," I said evenly, trying hard to figure this guy out. He was burly and rough-looking, with truly maniacal blue eyes. I followed his movements carefully as he walked toward the three hooded figures in the chairs. He pulled the hood off Schultzy, who was sweating profusely and breathing hard through his nose, as his mouth was taped shut.

"Good, Jack. We don't want anything to happen to our fellow cops. That's good." Dimitri stepped toward the person sitting in the third seat. "This fellow, for example, did not heed my advice, and so we are going to have to deal with him and his family."

He placed the nail gun on the third person's right foot and pulled the trigger twice. Pfoosh. The sickening pop sound of the nail tearing through the victim's foot was met by a muffled scream through his nose. He jumped, but didn't move very far because he was bound to the chair with uncomfortably tight-looking zip ties.

"You see, this may be a very bad night for this gentleman."

"Dimitri," I said, "I... I understand you are deadly serious; there's no need to do this—"

"Oh, Jack, but there is." Dimitri cut me off with his deep booming voice and proceeded to put two more nails into the third hostage's other foot. The poor guy screamed through his nose and shifted the chair over onto two legs, nearly toppling over, breathing very heavily and blood streaming out of his feet. Dimitri moved to the person in the center seat and placed the nail gun onto a much smaller foot, which caused the person to squirm and whimper through a taped mouth. Then, without dispensing a nail into the second person's foot, Dimitri moved to Schultzy and placed the nail gun on his left foot, eliciting a squirm and heavy nose breathing from him. I started to sweat as my pulse quickened, worried that Rocky might take over and put Schultzy and the hostages at risk. Anger kicks off the process. My muscles feel hot, then they lock up, my eyes narrow, then Rocky takes over. I have to remain calm as I sense Rocky just below the surface, a growing compulsion to act, move to take on the big man.

Dimitri threw the nail gun onto the floor and drew a pistol from behind his back, "So, Jack, I want you to take this cop and go tell the other cops to fuck off and leave us alone by the *top of the hour*. You going to do that?"

"Yes, Dimitri, I'm convinced. I'll get them to back off by the top of the hour," I said as I watched the pistol warily as his hand shook with a slight tremor.

"You got family?" Dimitri sneered, stepping close enough that his breath, which reeked of alcohol and coffee, stung me in the face as he pushed his pistol into my gut. "Maybe a lonely mother or a pretty sister? A nice little home somewhere? Just imagine...all the things that could happen if you cops don't back off." My muscles started to stiffen as I fought the urge to grab him by the throat.

"No, not yet," I said, trying to keep my responses short so I wouldn't inadvertently trip some unseen red line with this maniac.

"Okay, Jack, I'm in a hurry, so it's time for you to go. Oh, and I wouldn't want to have to put a lot of effort into finding your weak spot. You wouldn't like that, so don't piss me off. Russ, get this cop up. Sparks, quit screwing around with that and start packing up."

"Yes, boss," they replied. Russ swiftly moved around me and began cutting the zip ties holding Schultzy in his chair, while Dimitri moved back to stand eyeball to eyeball with me. His poise and expression almost dared me to try something, but I sensed something else occupying his mind. Desperation? Was he really as reckless as the Feds indicated? I couldn't get a good read on him.

Russ stood Schultzy up and walked him into the hallway while I stood nose-to-nose with an agitated murderer. I'm six feet, four inches tall and was still looking up an inch or two at this guy. I could see the violence gleaming in his eyes. I glanced down at the other hostage then resumed the staring contest with Dimitri.

*Don't do it, Jack. Schultzy is the op,* I thought to myself, rather loudly. *Too late, I've got to try and save them.*

"Any chance you can let that one come with me, too?" I asked calmly.

Dimitri glanced back toward the smaller hostage and then back, stepping even closer to me, pressing the pistol into my ribs. "No, Jack, that one is business-related," he whispered with fake sincerity. "It's a tight package, though. Maybe I'll have some fun with it when our business is complete. I'm such a lady's man, you know. Or maybe I'll do something more... interesting."

"Okay, well, I had to try," I said as his comments confirmed my guess that the second hostage was a female.

Dimitri barked orders to the remaining crew, "Sparks, get these two moving. We are leaving." The man named Sparks clipped the smaller hostages' zip ties and stood her up. Sparks pushed her a little too hard, causing her to fall forward onto the floor, the hood still in place. Dimitri stepped over and grabbed her by the shirt, picking her up off the floor with a single powerful motion. "Take it off. She can walk on her own," he said, pulling the hood off the woman as Sparks pushed her into the adjoining room. For an instant, she turned to look at me. I could see the sheer terror in her eyes. My heart stopped dead, frozen solid. I knew those emerald eyes and that brown hair. *It was Ginger.*

Rage instantly reignited inside me. I fought hard to push Rocky down. *How'd she get mixed up with these guys? Do they know about us? Did I get her into this somehow? I've got to get her out of here.*

# Chapter 2

Despite the rain, I pulled Chief Borland and Agent Jenkins out of the mobile headquarters bus and told them about the directive to leave by the top of the hour. They looked puzzled as Chief Borland returned my pistol, rain dripping from his outstretched arm down onto the Glock.

"There are six of them in there, including Dimitri Miokin. They are very well armed and knew we were here. They had two additional hostages, so a total of eight people in that suite."

I returned the sidearm to my holster and gestured toward Schultzy.

"I think one of the two hostages is an informant. He seems to know a lot about their operation, the police, and the Bureau's investigation," Sergeant Schultz said, looking at Agent Jenkins as water dripped from his nose.

Before Jenkins could respond, I jumped in. "I have a plan to get the hostages. Maybe get the bad guys, too, but it's thin. It will take some luck and a little sleight of hand."

Detective Angie Heist exited the mobile headquarters vehicle just in time to see Chief Borland glance down at his watch and say, "Okay, Jack, we have thirteen minutes. Let's hear it."

So I quickly laid out the plan.

Angie, nearly six feet tall, solid chin, dark skin, and large eyes, was first to chime in. "I don't think the mayor would approve of this plan,

Chief. It's risky."

I frowned at Angie, figuring she'd say something along those lines. I'd long suspected the mayor brought her into Wellspoint PD after the Mindjack Murders case to augment, and I think, keep an eye on things from the inside.

Schultzy spoke up, "I think it's worth a shot if they travel the likely route. It can work."

Agent Jenkins rubbed his chin, clearly thinking through the plan. "There are an awful lot of things that can go wrong, Jack."

"Look, in the middle of every shit situation lies an opportunity. This is a chance to catch this Dimitri dirtbag and get the hostages outta there. Besides, your snitch is dead if they move him to another location. They put two nails from a nail gun in each of his feet. This is the only way to have a chance at a rescue," I said, eyes darting between Jenkins and Chief Borland.

Chief Borland eyed Angie warily through the dark rain, apparently thinking about the mayor's perspective, then glancing at Agent Jenkins and Sergeant Schultz, then finally peering back at me. "I don't like it, Jack. It puts a lot more people at risk and we lose the element of—"

"Ginger Rowland is the second hostage," I said, cutting him off.

Chief's face twisted in a combination of anger and disbelief. "What? How'd Ginger get involved?"

"I don't know," I shrugged.

"She's an old friend of Detective Stewart and a friend to the force here at Wellspoint," Schultzy said to a puzzled Agent Jenkins, who nodded, resulting in gobs of water dumping from pockets that formed in his boonie hat. He exhaled deeply, taking off his hat and running his hand through thick locks of wet blond hair hanging down to his shoulders. He definitely didn't look like a prototypical special agent. At five foot, five, he probably weighed 150 pounds soaking wet, as he was right now.

"We have to try," I said, looking at Chief Borland.

me into a locker at the YMCA. Threatened to beat my ass. The night I arrested his son still haunts me. I nearly killed that kid and then sent him to prison." I replied, recalling how Rocky roughed up the stoned attacker that fateful night in April.

My words hung in the air unanswered.

Oli lowered his head perceptibly and replied, "Drugs took that kid over; you probably saved his life."

I looked at Oli, then shifted my gaze over to Tower. They returned the look, both with solemn, tiny nods.

Sixty quiet seconds elapsed as we all looked at different Television screens.

Tower raised a hand, signaling our location, and thirty very long, quiet seconds later, a waitress arrived with three cheeseburger baskets, fries, and a cup of decaf coffee.

"Okay, gents, dinner is on me, Jack," Tower said, "here's our best decaf. It's that fancy stuff, the bean you showed me on Instagram."

"Thanks, Tower, smells great," I said, grabbing the coffee cup and sniffing its rich aroma. I smiled at the waitress, Rachael, as she winked at me.

"Good to see you, Jack, hope you enjoy the coffee."

"Thank you, Rachael. It smells wonderful."

"Agreed, thank you, T-dog, this is perfect," Oli replied.

Oli contorted his face at the smell of the coffee. "I don't know how you drink that stuff. It smells terrible."

"Hey, this is mankind's most revered drink, Oli, you don't know what you are missing."

Oli shook his head back and forth, "Just nasty, that's all I can say."

"Eat your cheeseburger, you cretin," I said, nodding and smiling at Tower as I sipped my coffee.

We silently dug into the food and started watching the game, occasionally clapping and cheering, our emotions ebbing and flowing with those of the many fans in the bar.

"Jack, maybe you could just check on her boyfriend, just size up the situation. From there, I could probably handle it," said Oli.

Tower stopped chewing mid-fry and looked from Oli to me with high eyebrows.

I glanced at Tower as he ever so slightly shook his head from side to side at me.

Thirty long seconds passed as we all watched the game.

I exhaled fully and glanced at Oli, "Okay, Oli, I'll look into the boyfriend. Do *not* tell Sarah anything."

"Outstanding, Jack!" Oli said with a massive grin on his face. He took out a pen and wrote the boyfriend's name on one of his business cards. "This is the guy, Jonas Crutchfield, who works over at Adrenaline Autos."

I took the card and put it in my pocket. "No guarantees, Oli, I'm just going to check in on him, nothing further. Does Becker know this guy is beating her up? I suppose that's a dumb question."

"No. And I want to keep it that way." Oli replied with a nod and a tight smile. "She blames her dad for her brother going to prison, so she got mad and left home. Becker reached out to me and asked for a favor."

"Nice of you to help, sure, I get it, I wouldn't want Becker to know his little girl was getting beat up on my watch either. Is she aware that you know her father?" I asked

"I think she knows something's there, but does not know I'm helping him by giving her a job. She had just graduated from high school and was planning to move away to make Becker angry, but this job opportunity arose, which has kept her local. It's a computer science job, and that's what she's interested in. She's a freaking coding prodigy, a real whiz, who's already racked up awards for her skills in programming and digital security. And that's what Becker asked for. Help him keep her local until he can repair their relationship."

I started to think about the potential disaster confrontation that would occur if Becker found out I was involved in any way with his daughter. I tried to push that away and focus on the game.

After a very quiet few minutes, Tower stuffed the last bit of hamburger into his mouth and, with a muffled voice, said, "Topic change, why do you have two cell phones, Jack?"

"This one is Schultzy's," I said, stuffing down a few French fries with one hand and lifting one of the two cell phones sitting on the table next to my food basket. "He should be back tomorrow morning, so Chief Borland asked me to give it back to him as I'd likely see him first."

Both Tower and Oli's heads bobbed up and down in acknowledgment as their attention was drawn to the TVs by a rise in voices within the room. Cheers broke out as the Reds' third baseman, Skyler Perez, hit a towering, 400-foot home run over center field that put the Reds up by three runs. I conservatively pumped a fist in anticipation of a win against the vaunted L.A. Dodgers, a team that's won more than its share of pennants in my humble opinion.

It was about thirty minutes later that I noticed on my watch that I'd received a text message from Special Agent Jenkins. Two messages, actually, so I grabbed both phones and said, "Seems like this one is over; I'm going to get out of here and head home. Thanks for dinner, Tower, it hit the spot." I grabbed the baseball out of my pocket and held it up to Oli, "Thanks, Oli, that was a nice gift, a fantastic bit of memorabilia." They both grunted and nodded affirmatively, each bumping my fist as they continued to focus on the game.

On my way out, I pinged a ride service on my cell phone, the screen's glow momentarily harsh against the dimly lit sidewalk. The familiar chime of the app was soothing as I started walking down the street, the damp pavement slick beneath my shoes. A text message alert had popped up on my screen, a little bubble of light I barely registered. I didn't get a chance to read it.

A dark sedan, almost black, with four doors, rolled up next to me, the hum of its engine a low, insistent drone that demanded my attention. The headlights sliced through the twilight, momentarily blinding me. I reached for my phone to double-check the rideshare app, a reflex I should have avoided.

"You, Jack Stewart?" the driver asked, his voice flat, devoid of any warmth. It felt rehearsed.

"Yep, that's me," I answered, trying to keep my voice even, betraying nothing.

A second person got out of the front passenger door. He moved with a silent efficiency that was deeply unsettling. He was shrouded in shadow, but the glint of metal caught the light as he pointed a pistol with a long, ominous silencer attached to the barrel directly at me. Just two words, delivered with chilling detachment: "Get in."

I glanced back up the street. A few people milled around in front of the pub entrance, their laughter and chatter distant and meaningless. I wasn't going to get anyone's attention before this guy could shoot me from ten feet away. My gut twisted with tension, and the air suddenly felt thick and suffocating. A cold certainty settled over me. *This wasn't a ride to share.*

So, I got in the car. The door closed with a soft, unsettling click, sealing my fate.

# Chapter 7

"What can I do for you boys?" I said as calmly as possible, wiggling into the back seat behind the driver.

"Give me your pistol, real slow," the passenger said as he turned in the front seat, continuing to point his monster pistol back at me. I slowly handed him my Glock as we drove down the street and finally turned onto a side street where we rolled up to another car with two people standing behind it.

The passenger got out and was immediately replaced by another pistol-wielding male, wearing a hat and gloves, apparently named Antonio, a big fellow with dark features who spoke with an accent. It was a language I couldn't quite place, maybe Portuguese. "Where's his gun and cell phone?" Antonio said over his shoulder.

I kept quiet, not sure how to navigate this little adventure just yet.

"Give me your phone," said Antonio with a heavy Latin accent.

"This seems to be a substandard ride share service; most don't ask for my personal effects," I said as I handed him my cell phone.

He glared at me. Then took my phone and pistol in his other hand, then handed them out the window to another person while watching me intently with his pistol trained on my torso. "Take these to his house, throw them in his backyard." A few minutes later, the other car departed while we drove off as well, but the kidnappers remained silent.

"Look, kidnapping a police officer is a serious offense—"

"Shut up. I was told to bring you in alive. They didn't say I couldn't shoot you in the knees," the big man said.

*Noted*, I thought sarcastically.

We started driving north out of town, and it got a little darker in the car, with no streetlights around. I decided to use this to my advantage. I shifted around in the back seat, pretending to adjust my pants and scratch my elbow, all of which caused the big guy to focus on me more intently for a moment, then his attention drifted. I managed to fish Schultzy's cell phone out of my back pocket and thumb around trying to make a call by pressing the call button behind my back, not sure if it was working. *Crap.* We rolled up to an old warehouse building, and the car stopped. I quickly jammed the phone down into the crease between the bench part of the seat and the backrest.

"Get out," said the big man, just as a person who had exited the warehouse opened my door.

"Okay, okay, take it easy," I said, holding up my hands and stepping out of the vehicle.

With a shotgun pointed right at me, the new guy motioned for me to go through the door in the warehouse where he had just exited. Just as I walked through the door, I took a big punch to the chin. I stumbled forward, reaching for my assailant, but only tripped to the floor, landing on my hands and knees. *Okay, now it's real,* I thought.

"Pick 'em up!" I heard. "Get him in the chair."

I recognized that voice. Groggy from the powerful punch, it took me a few minutes to gather myself. My muscles felt hot, then started locking up as my eyes narrowed and the dark cloud crept all around me. I felt Rocky step in, and I lost control.

*Large, empty, high-ceilinged room, rolling cabinets and broken furniture, not much else within view. The room is mostly dark, with portable lights shining on me. Lots of cables and wires are lying everywhere. Twelveish steps from the entryway located at 7:00 behind me, five attackers, two leaders, cooperative status unknown. Hands are now bound behind my back, sitting in an armless chair with my shoes removed, my feet in a wide pan of something that looks like water,* thought Rocky.

One of the men threw a bucket of water on me. It was shockingly cold, clinging to my skin like a second layer of ice. "Wake up, Jack, it's time to have a little talk." The water smelled faintly of rust and something vaguely chemical, a metallic tang clinging to the back of my throat.

*There's that voice again.* I opened my eyes fully to see Dimitri Miokin standing over me. The bright portable lights cast unforgiving light, highlighting the grime smeared across his face and the cold glint in his blue eyes. The air hung thick and heavy with the smell of damp concrete, oil, and a distant plant smell I couldn't quite place, something artificial, like overripe fruit left to rot. The space around me felt vast and echoing, a cavernous room filled with the silhouettes of hulking machinery.

"Now let me tell you what pretty shit you are in, so hopefully this can go easier. I need you to tell me how much you cops know about Christina."

"Christina, who?" I grunted, testing my bonds. The zip ties chafed raw against my wrists, leaving angry red marks on my skin as I tested them. A single drop of water traced a slow path down my temple, tasting metallic on my lips.

"That was the wrong answer, Jack." Dimitri said as he looked back over his shoulder, held up his right hand with two fingers extended into the air and yelled, "Give him two seconds."

Pain seared through my body as electricity slammed through my feet, through my torso, causing me to jerk uncontrollably. The smell of ozone, sharp and acrid, filled the air as the current surged. My muscles locked, every nerve screaming. *Okay, that was some decent amperage; can't take much of that. Better engage and shift topics,* thought Rocky.

"So this is payback?" I grunted, looking down at my feet in a flat pan of fluid, then looking back at Dimitri, "You run out of nail guns?"

"I'm expecting a new nail gun in about an hour, but yes, payback. Spake is one of mine. I also want to know what you know about Christina. My people have learned that submerging your victim's feet in water creates an uncomfortable and vulnerable position, making them more susceptible to psychological manipulation." He squatted down and peered into my eyes with that crazy, madman stare and twisted grin. "I warned you. Look, Jack, no one knows where you are, and we have a long night of pain planned for you if you don't tell me what you know."

"I'm telling you the truth, I don't know anyone named Christina."

"Make it four seconds this time," Dimitri yelled over his shoulder.

Wham, the pain seared through my body again as it jerked uncontrollably. When the electricity stopped, saliva drooled out of my mouth, and I shook my head to try and clear it and collect my thoughts. Dimitri must have gotten bored as he'd walked away toward the person in charge of shocking me.

I failed to answer correctly two more times before I nearly passed out. During the shocks, I took stock of how much I could move my body. *Hands are bound, but just to each other, not to the chair. My feet were bound together, but I could move my left foot fairly well, lifting it out of the pan of water or whatever was down there. The right foot is not as loose, and I think it is somehow bound to the chair or the ground.* I must have freed my left foot during the shock sessions. I heard numerous steps and Dimitri's voice distantly from across the room. He sounded like he was multitasking.

"Is he awake? Ask him again."

Antonio was bending over me, looking at me to see if I was conscious. At least I think it was Antonio. My sight was clouded. He kept leaning over and looking into my face. *Here we go. Time to move, thought* Rocky.

Antonio asked me about Christina. I played dead. Hell, I felt close to death. Electrocution does that. *Have one chance here, gotta make it work.* I wearily raised my head and said, "Christina Aguilera?"

"Hit him with some more, he's asking for it," said Antonio.

I heard Dimitri's voice in the distance, "Okay, hit him with five seconds."

In the blink of an eye, I put my left foot under the large pan containing probably water and flipped it up into Antonio's direction. He noticed it too late. He, too, was filled with a massive jolt of electricity, only he wasn't expecting it. At all. The electricity stopped, and Antonio fell over onto me, rocking me backwards in the chair, slamming me onto the floor with a dazed Antonio on top of me.

I squirmed off the chair and pushed Antonio aside in a split second. I heard men yelling to one another and footsteps heading my way as I rolled onto my side, pulled my bound hands under my butt, down to my feet to bring them in front of my body. My right foot was still zip-tied to the chair, so with both hands and my free foot, I twisted my bound foot against the chair and snapped the zip tie.

Rolling back to the left, I pull a stunned but recovering Antonio back toward me. *Let's see you shoot somebody in the knees with a broken Arm,* quipped Rocky as I twisted my legs around his torso, pulling his gun hand up into a perfect arm bar - Snap! I could see pain distort his face as he instinctively twisted away from me. I reached over and picked up his gun, then pointed it into his face. Weary from being shocked, I slid backwards as he slowly raised his hands and shook his head.

Movement caught my eye to the left as I saw Dimitri and another bad guy running my way. When they saw me with the pistol, they stopped and took cover behind broken warehouse equipment. I fired two rounds in their direction and then shot two of the bright spotlights while surveying the scene. I could see the bad guy out the door window heading toward the door, so I shot in his direction through the window.

I jumped to my bare feet and bolted across the dark warehouse room, looking for defensible cover or concealment that would give me some space to think and maneuver. I heard what sounded like three loud pops as somebody started shooting in my direction, and I could hear bullets ricocheting far away from me. *I'm toast if I can't get out of this room, need some advantage or high ground*, I thought.

As I neared the furthest wall, I saw a narrow service ladder that appeared to go up to the third floor and onward. I could hear more bullets ring out as I scurried up the ladder. There was no access to the second floor; I could see it, but it was wire-screened off. As soon as I made it to the third floor, a set of weak lights turned on in the warehouse, illuminating my escape. More bullets, but impacting much closer this time.

"Get up there," I heard Dimitri order someone. Crouching for a moment, I pulled the magazine out of my pistol and counted eight rounds left.

*Need to conserve ammo.* I deftly stuck my head out over the freshly lit maintenance ladder to get a glimpse of how many folks were inbound. A single military-aged male, climbing with a pistol in his right hand. I looked around and found a tool tray with several wrenches, sockets, and such. I grabbed the tray and toolbox and dropped them parallel to the service ladder. The heavy items made a clunking sound as they struck the bad guy, followed by several clangs as the individual tools dispersed, striking objects on their way to the floor, along with the sound of a loud thump as the assailant hit the ground.

To the left, about 300 feet away, on the other side of the dark room, I heard footsteps banging against thin metal stairs. I was about to have company. The lights were not on in this room, so I couldn't see clearly, but I did see motions and shadows. Three assailants, each with at least a single handgun.

I shifted left and moved behind a large conveyor belt motor just as an object came skidding toward me across the wooden floor. There was a loud sound, like a firework too close, and a blinding light, as I realized it was a flashbang grenade. My ears were ringing from the grenade as I fired two more rounds and moved to a new position behind what looked like a saw table and cabinets of some sort. I started taking fire from two locations, but I couldn't make them out exactly. *Time to move again,* I thought. I fired two more rounds and backed all the way to the rear wall, kneeling on the ground.

I glanced to my left and saw a faintly illuminated EXIT sign about fifteen feet away, so I crawled to a new position where I could see the door, which appeared to be an emergency exit. I jumped to my knees, then onto one knee, fired two more rounds, and then bolted for the door. I slammed into the door with my shoulder, and a loud metallic womp sound. It didn't freakin' open. *Holy Crap!*

Bullets became hail, striking all around me. On my knees, I noticed a massive stack of paint cans and thought about hiding behind them. I glanced back at the door and realized I hadn't hit the emergency release bar. *Crap!* I reached up and pushed the unlock bar, and the door creaked open. I grabbed two paint cans and rolled them aggressively down the walkway in an attempt to distract the assailants. I rolled out the door and pushed it closed. I turned and sprinted along the narrow fire escape walkway in a crouch. The walkway led back to the front of the building. There was no way down, no stairs or even a step ladder. *Crap!*

I heard the door I'd just come through slam open and footsteps banging away on the narrow walkway behind me. Out of the corner of my eye, I noticed movement below in front of the main entryway of the building. Bad guys popped out and started shooting at me, so I crouched down, considering possible courses of action. I was officially trapped, with nowhere to go, and bad guys moving in around me from multiple directions.

I crouched down even lower, preparing to fire at the men heading my way from the fire escape pathway; luckily, they were single file due to the walkway's narrow width.

That's when I heard multiple inbound rounds. Big rounds, zipping by and making loud impacts into the metal walls. *Whoa. Rifle shots.* I lay flat and craned my neck around, trying to get a bead on where those new rounds were coming from. They continued to hit the walls like birds flying into a glass window. The shooter appeared to be targeting the bad guys both below and above. The bad guys on the narrow walkway receded into the building as the door was rocked with high-velocity rifle rounds.

"Schultzy!" I said aloud to no one in particular. In the distance, behind the parked cars, up the driveway, I could see a faintly colored red light with occasional bright muzzle bursts. Maybe someone did see me get kidnapped; maybe the ride-share driver saw everything.

"Jack, let's go!" A faint voice whispered from below. "Jack, get your big ass down here, jump into the trees and climb down."

*Who the hell is that?* I thought. That wasn't Schultzy's voice. More volleys of powerful rifle shots pounded into the metal structure. Schultzy must have been holding the bad guys' attention so this person could get close. I started hearing popping sounds as the bad guys apparently started firing back at a distant Schultzy.

I looked at the trees near the corner of the building. I could barely make out that they were basically mature scrub trees surrounding a good-sized maple or oak tree. The larger limbs shifted in the slight breeze, just out of reach. Not many strong-looking branches, though.

I got to my feet and considered how far off the narrow walkway I'd have to jump to make the trees. *Holy Crap, I can't believe I'm doing this!*

# Chapter 8

"Here goes nothing," I murmured to myself and took four giant steps, placed my right hand on the rail and pulled both feet up onto the handrail for a millisecond before leaping into the maple tree. Unfortunately, it was so dark with only faint light from a nearby security lamp that I missed grabbing the large limb I was aiming for.

I managed to grab a smaller limb that slowed my fall. Until it broke. And then I started falling ass-first into the remaining limbs, finally catching one that smacked me painfully across my back, flipping me over so the next branch down could wack me in the head. "Shit!" I managed to hang on to this one and carefully slipped down the maple tree. Then bullets started ricocheting around me, so I just let go and fell the rest of the way to the ground, landing on my left side with an awkward thud.

"Jack, let's goooo!" the muffled and distorted voice nearby said. I think it sounded that way because I had taken a shot to the noggin and had been, you know, electrocuted, so I was moving slowly. Blood streamed into my face from a huge cut over my right eye. I was struggling to pull it together, moving slowly. I got onto all fours and started crawling out of the patch of trees and brush.

Someone grabbed my left hand and pulled hard as if they were trying to stand me up. Then the person put my left arm over their shoulder and lifted me into a hunched position, and then we started shuffling in the direction of Schultzy. My rescuer was struggling to drag me along, but we were moving. I winced in pain over and over again as I kept stepping on sticks, rocks and other sharp things in the grass as we headed down the side of the drive.

*Well, crap*, I thought, *I could really use some shoes here.* A smell on this person was stinging me back to reality. What was it? It smelled like a weak perfume. I swear the scent was energizing me. So I started stepping more independently, "Goooo!" the voice said in an all-out scream. We were both sprinting while under fire from the bad guys back in the warehouse building.

"Over here," yelled Schultzy as we shifted our path toward the voice. Ten more steps, and we ran right past Schultzy and slid to the ground behind him. Then we crawled back over to the cover that Schultzy had found.

"Nice of you to escape, Jack. I thought I was going to have to put on a pizza delivery uniform and come in to get you!" Schultzy said from behind a concrete pillar that was part of the driveway gate system. He continued taking shots at the bad guys with his SR-25 sniper rifle.

I panted heavily, "Thank you, Schultzy, much appreciated; it's been a helluva day."

"Don't thank me, thank Angie, she took all the real risks."

*Angie?* I looked over and under the faint moonlight, and I saw a smiling Angie Heist huffing and puffing for air. "Thank you. Damn, I certainly owe you one. A *big one.* Anything, you name it."

Angie smiled at me, "Sorry, Jack, I don't date cops. Schultzy, we gotta get out of here; there's at least four or five of them, and they'll be coming."

"Where'd you get that training?" I said, grinning and breathing hard.

"United States Marine Corps," she replied, still breathing heavily herself.

Schultzy gathered his rifle and kit, then started heading for the truck. "Well, they won't be coming in those two vehicles in front of the building because I took out the tires and windshields. Come on, you two, we've got to get outta here."

We jumped into Schultzy's F-150 and drove down the long twisty driveway, finally turning onto the highway heading back toward the city of Wellspoint.

"I don't know how you two saved me, but I'm very grateful," I said from the back seat. Schultzy drove like a madman as Angie grabbed for her bag.

"Here, put this on that gash on your forehead; it looks pretty bad. You are bleeding everywhere," Angie said, shaking her head and handing me a folded-up T-shirt.

"Yeah, no bleeding in my truck," quipped Schultzy

"Thank you," was all I could respond with. I felt truly terrible: my head was pounding, and blood was seeping into my right eye, making it burn. My lip was split and bleeding from the warehouse door punch, although the feeling of nausea from all of the shocks was starting to abate, thankfully. More importantly, I managed to keep Rocky mostly under control. I picked all the debris from my feet and fell back into the corner of the seat and door, exhausted and holding the t-shirt on my forehead.

"How did you know where I was?" I asked with a slight slur in my speech.

"Chief Borland called me. He said he'd received several calls from Schultzy's phone and figured something was wrong since he'd just given it to you."

"She called me," Schultzy started, "and I had a feeling something was screwed up, so we did some checking, triangulated my phone with cell tower data, and it led us to the old Browning warehouse. They used to make parts for airplanes and soda machines, that sort of thing, but it's been closed down for quite a while, so no good reason for you to be there."

"Jack, did you receive the group text from Special Agent Jenkins?" Angie said.

"I did see it, but the assholes back there got my attention before I could read it. What did it say?"

Schultzy looked over at Angie, and then she turned back to look at me from the front seat, "he said, 'Code blue, criminals on the loose,' and that was it. I called him back but got no answer."

"Okay, that's not good. Maybe the bad guys went after him, too?" I replied.

"Very possible."

An alert came over Angie's radio indicating an officer had been assaulted and was being taken to the Wellspoint Hospital. Angie asked for the officer's name, and the reply left us all stunned.

"The officer was Chief Borland," I overheard from her radio.

The escalating chaos from the coordinated attacks on Bureau field office personnel to the ambushes on Wellspoint police painted a grim picture. It was becoming chillingly clear that someone had orchestrated a synchronized attack, diverting resources and exploiting vulnerabilities in both the Bureau and Wellspoint police departments with unsettling precision.

"Schultzy—" I started.

The truck started accelerating aggressively as Schultzy replied, "We are on our way to the hospital, Jack. I was taking you there anyway."

Angie and I compared notes on the bad guys, while Schultzy described how thankful he was that his wife and son were safely out of reach.

"I need some shoes," I commented under my breath.

"Jack, my gym bag is back there somewhere. Why don't you try my basketball shoes; see if they fit? " said Schultzy.

"Thanks, I'll give them a try; my feet are kind of mangled," I replied.

I looked around and pulled out a pair of brightly colored high-top basketball shoes from his bag. I fished around for some socks.

Even with my feet covered, the echo of the electricity still vibrated beneath my skin. It would take more than a moment to right myself, but the Chief was in trouble and that demanded every ounce of my focus. My mind struggled to untangle the threads of criminal conspiracy interwoven with familiar concerns for the Chief and Ginger, as well as the release from Rocky. "We've got to get ahead of these bastards, seize the initiative," I growled to Schultzy and Angie. The words felt brittle, a shield against the fear coiling in my twisting gut because if the Chief was truly in danger, these weren't just criminals. They were a threat to everything we stood for.

* * *

We burst through the emergency room doors, and the antiseptic stench hit us like an unearned slap in the face. The dimly lit lobby was a sea of modern but worn furniture and weary patients, each with their faces contorted by worry or fatigue. Beeping machines, crying children, and muffled conversations distracted me as I spoke with the nurse to gather details about the Chief and get my head stitched up. The nurse said that Chief Borland was being evaluated and was unconscious. She took a look at me and moved me into a room for treatment while Schultzy and Angie headed for the waiting area outside the Chief's room.

Ninety minutes later, I stumbled out of the treatment room, trying to put events into perspective.

"Holy cow, you look like shit, you okay?" Schultzy asked wide-eyed as I entered the small waiting area.

"Oh yes, stitches are my specialty. Feeling much better now. I got eight stitches over my eyebrow and two stitches in my lip. And some drugs to deal with my feet." I replied, plopping down into the chair next to Angie and sipping on some electrolyte drink.

"We thought you were going to be held overnight. We were just about to leave. Louie sent Sergeant Capwell over to provide security for the Chief tonight," Angie said.

"Still unconscious?" I replied, looking toward the Chief's room. We could see him in the hospital bed through the doorway. A mountain of a man, Sergeant Capwell walked up and down the hallway outside the door, looking back toward us occasionally and smiling.

"He's been in and out of it. Doctors think he got a nasty concussion, but he is looking much better. They want him to rest tonight under observation. Apparently, his car was run off the road in a particularly perilous place. His car rolled down a huge embankment," Schultzy said.

Angie nodded and then chimed in, "Special Agent Jenkins was released from the hospital about thirty minutes ago. He's taking his family into protective custody. He was shot three times in a firefight outside his home. Apparently, a tougher mark than what attackers considered. He shot one of the assailants, killing him."

"Special Agent Charlie Jenkins, your family, Chief, and me. A well-planned, simultaneous attack on cops," I replied as Angie and Schultzy nodded affirmatively.

We sat quietly for a time.

Angie and Schultzy stood. "You want a ride home?" he asked.

I looked at Schultzy, then over to Angie. I gritted my teeth and then looked over at the Chief in his bed with monitors and systems beeping and chirping in a soothing rhythm. I stood and replied solemnly, "No, I'll grab a ride share later. I'm grateful for you both saving my ass. Thank you." I looked into Angie's eyes with a raised eyebrow, "I owe you one. A big one."

Angie stuck out her hand and smiled.

So I shook it and smiled back. A genuine smile that rushed into my weary eyes.

"Hey now, don't expect to get repaid. In fact, don't borrow or trade with him for anything; he'll never repay you. The guy still owes me for an entire crate of M&Ms I got for him at Forward Operating Base Granite. You just can't get quality candy like that in the Middle East. It was worth hundreds," Schultzy snickered as I looked at him and smiled, shaking my head from left to right.

I went into the Chief's room and stood over him, looking around at the gadgets surrounding the bed. He was wired up to at least four different systems, each beeping and clicking along rhythmically. I exhaled deeply, rubbing my chin, and looked around the room in survey mode. I dragged a chair near the bed and pulled the corner table holding ancient magazines into range of my feet. I sat down and started talking to him as the deputy walked back and forth in the hallway.

"Hang in there, boss, we need you back in the game so we can sort out how to handle these criminals. You'd have been proud of Angie and Schultzy; they dug me out of a pretty deep hole over at Brownie's warehouse. It was Miokin and his crew. They must have some solid backing to so brazenly take on cops. They are not screwing around, and they seem wound up about someone named Christina." I shifted in my seat, thinking about what the Chief would say after my comments and continued, "Yes, I managed to keep Rocky under control... this time."

I talked through the day pretending Chief Borland was listening. A huge part of me was hoping his gravelly voice would spring to life, telling me what to do next and how to get this situation under control. No such luck.

*Who in the hell is Christina? And why do these criminals care about a small town in Ohio?* My mind reeled through connections, but nothing seemed to link together. I started to put a couple of events together, not sure they belonged that way, but they fit. I needed to think through those odd occurrences.

# Chapter 9

"You're late, detective," said the deputy mayor with his arms folded across his chest and green eyes blazing with annoyance. At five feet ten, with blond hair, a cleft chin, sandy brown hair, and a pinstriped suit with creases that looked like a bulldozer had pressed them, he looked the part of a politician. Neat, well-spoken. The Chief had called him a key resource for the mayor. A resource clever enough to get out of messes, or make them, I suppose.

The room smelled like coffee, Pine-Sol, and sweat; fluorescent lights hummed overhead, brightening the room enough to see everyone clearly. "I was at the hospital, checking on Chief Borland," I said while scanning the room to find Angie, who fidgeted in her chair, her eyes darting between the deputy mayor and me, then looking away.

"Yes, we've all been briefed on the events from last night. There's a great deal to go over. Everyone else is dismissed. I'd like to speak with Detective Stewart in private."

*We've been briefed, huh?* I thought, remembering an image of Chief Borland lying helplessly in a hospital bed.

Everyone filed from the room as the deputy mayor stood ten feet away, looking me up and down.

"Dr. Davies approached the mayor from the university. She indicated that you've been '*Investigating*' for a long time, and she isn't aware of any evidence of foul play. She wants us to officially close the case so they can clear the issue with their board and investors. Have you found any evidence of murder?"

"I haven't yet, but I'm not done running down the final leads. It'll be done in a couple more days."

"Okay, you have until noon tomorrow to find evidence, or we're closing the case. The mayor has a media roundtable at the university tomorrow at 2 p.m. and wants to close this out, so that's the deadline. We need to start acting with urgency around here."

"Sir, I'm not sure I'll have all the data analysis complete to—"

"Detective, you do know how to follow orders, correct? I mean, you can do what you are told without blowing up half the city or inadvertently killing half of its citizens?"

I considered his statement and the situation with Dr. Davies. "I'll get you an answer by noon," I acquiesced, shuffling my aching feet around. Schultzy's shoes were a half size too small, and the cuts on my soles were still bleeding, making a rather stinky, sockless foot sauce.

"You appear unfit to serve today. And what's with those obnoxious basketball shoes? They smell like they've been in a dumpster," he sneered, condescension dripping from every word.

My eyes blazed with irritation as I fought to control my response to questions from a bureaucrat with zero operational experience in investigating crime or police work in general. "Regarding the investigation, there are inconsistencies with some evidence, which is slowing me down. Regarding the shoes, given the circumstances, I had to take what I could get," I replied, glancing down at the neon yellow, Lambert series high-topped basketball shoes and then shrugging my shoulders.

The deputy mayor snorted again, rolling his eyes in disgust. "You're a disgrace, Stewart. A reckless cad whose actions and inactions ruin our reputation with our citizens." His voice rose an octave higher as he took a step closer. "And don't even get me started on the damage you've caused to public property during your *investigations*. The assault accusations. Thousands of city dollars down the drain because of your incompetence!"

I felt my temper rising, "What is it with you? What is your beef with me? I've continually gotten the job done over and over—"

The deputy mayor cut me off with a mocking laugh. "Oh, please. You're just lucky I don't fire you on the spot for your constant screw-ups. There's no Chief Borland here to save you."

"We are into something big here; we need to pull the team together and figure out the next steps," I replied, raising my voice by an octave.

The deputy mayor rolled his eyes, dropped his arms to his side and took a few steps closer, finally placing his hands on his hips. "I want to be crystal clear. I'm in charge now, Stewart. The first step here is to clean up this organization and make it operate efficiently, and put some proper oversight into place. And know I'm watching you closely. It's just a matter of time before you screw up again, and when you do, I'm going to remove you for cause. *You* caused the attack on federal agents; *you* are the reason Sergeant Schultz's family is in protective custody, and *you* put Troy Borland in that hospital. You are responsible for this entire damned mess. How many innocent victims will die because of your erratic behavior? Just like your behavior on the disastrous Mindjack Murders case."

My gut twisted with irritation as I fired back, "No, sir, criminals put those people into those situations. I—"

"That's enough, detective. I don't want to hear your bullshit quibbling. Now, I want you to file your report and get the hell out of here. I intend to clean up this station and put some order into this place, and it starts today," said the deputy mayor with an increasingly flushed face.

My blood boiled as I glowered back at the Deputy, working hard not to clench my fists.

"You are dismissed, detective," the deputy exclaimed with eyes locked onto mine.

"Detective. *Detective!*" I heard the words from the door. "Detective, I need your help," said Schultzy from the open doorway.

I turned and looked at Schultzy. He waved me toward him. I turned back to the deputy mayor, who didn't move a muscle. Finally, I turned and left the room, walking with Schultzy back to my office. "Thanks" was all I could say.

In my office, Schultzy grabbed my left forearm, "Jack, I saw him publicly ripping into Sergeant Bartlett about an hour ago in the watch office for failing to send the morning status report to him on time. Geez, Jack, Sergeant Bartlett is the most consistent, responsible officer in this place. Things around here are going to fall apart without Chief Borland."

I glanced at my watch, then pulled Schultzy's hand off my forearm into my right hand, then pulled him into a half-hug, then pushed him back, "Don't worry, we've got this under control. Please let me know if you hear any updates about Chief Borland. I've got to get moving."

So I submitted a very short report and strode out of the station.

* * *

I pushed open the door of the retro diner as the bell above the door jingled hello to everyone for me. I was famished from being on the go for the past two days, and the place looked to be just what the doctor ordered. The highway-bound, isolated restaurant had a long service counter edged with mushroom-shaped, red stools with chrome bottoms along one side, and red vinyl-upholstered booths lined the opposite side of the single room joint. The place smelled of grease and strong Colombian coffee, and had shiny checkerboard flooring with nostalgic celebrity photos, Cincinnati Reds memorabilia, and Ohio-themed items displayed across all the walls.

I scanned the room, noting two waitresses and a handful of patrons. It was quiet, but I could hear the clinking of forks and knives against plates as the sizzle of cooking food emanated from the kitchen through the order pickup window. I moved toward the booth at the remote end of the diner, away from most of the other customers.

"Hi, Jack."

"Charlie," I nodded affirmatively with a half-smile, "Good to see you are still in one piece," I said, taking the opposite seat in the booth.

Charlie looked like I felt. He had a bruised right eye socket with a patch over it, seven or eight stitches through the right side of his chin, bruised right cheekbone, a scabbed-over lower lip, and that perennial smile on his face. He's a principled man who likes to do hard things. Surviving an attack from four paid killers meets that criteria. Folders were laid open as he was clearly reviewing evidence or reports of some kind.

"You want food?"

"I'm starving," I replied.

Charlie waved down the waitress, and I placed an order for steak and eggs, toast, and black coffee.

"Be careful with that stuff, it'll put hair on your saddle horn," Charlie said, smiling as I received the steaming hot cup of coffee from the waitress. She was about five feet tall with long brown hair rolled into a bun on the back of her head, an engaging smile, and eyes that seemed a little too far apart, creating an odd asymmetry to her face.

"That's right, the cook, Joey, well, he likes it strong. I think it's because he works twelve-hour shifts in here and needs it strong to keep up the work. A lot of our customers go with tea. Just saying," the waitress said.

"Relax, you two, I'm a *flexible* coffee connoisseur," I said as I took a big, confident sip of the coffee. My eyes immediately watered, and I fought back a choke. It tasted like someone boiled and filtered used transmission fluid from a city bus. *Holy Crap, it's strong coffee*, I thought, as my forced smile shifted into a disgusted pucker. I set the cup down gently on the grey vinyl tabletop.

We glanced at one another for about fifteen seconds before I replied, "Maybe, just bring me a half a cup of hot water too, it'll be alright after I cut it." I said cocking my head to the side.

Charlie laughed in pain, then chuckled, shaking his head from left to right, as the waitress said, "No problem, sweetie, I'll bring it right out."

"You okay?" I asked as I smiled at Charlie's pain-filled laugh.

"Oh, I took a .38 caliber shot to the chest, my vest stopped the round, but man did it make my ribs sore," he said through a grimace, rubbing the right side of his chest.

I leaned forward and lowered my head an inch, looking into Charlie's eyes. "What is going on? What kind of situation are we in here? These guys are hitting cops, federal agents, and going after families. They must have protection. Judges, that sort of thing? I need you to level with me, Charlie."

Charlie's grin drained away as he looked down at the tabletop, then raised his eyes to look at me intently. "Schultzy told me they tortured you, asked you about a person you didn't recognize. Christina?"

"Yes, a woman named Christina. No last name. By the way, Miokin personally supervised my *interview*. He mentioned how submerging my feet in water would increase the psychological terror effects of shocking me. Freakin Criminals don't do that, Charlie. You know who does? Professional fixers and hitmen. What are we into here?"

"I couldn't find anything on anyone named Christina, first or last name, related to this mess. Damn it!" Charlie said, gritting his teeth, "Hey, I told you he's a sadistic murderer."

"I got that. But what's his angle? What are you guys after him for besides murder? Kidnapping? Running Guns? There's no way the low-level criminals we've got in Wellspoint are driving this level of violence and energy. Something else is going on. What is it?"

Charlie looked away, staring at a distant point. He sipped his diluted coffee and replied, "Miokin is more than just a hired gun, but we can't figure out what he's doing in Wellspoint. He's in and out of New York City often, but never this far into the Midwest. He's affiliated with the Union organized crime organization."

"Union?" I replied.

"Yes.  Hard-core criminals who typically operate in Europe.  We became very concerned when Dimitri showed up in Ohio."

"I can see why. What are they into? Drugs? Guns?" I replied.

Charlie's quarter smile melted away, "Money. They steal it, transport it, convert it, or manage it for select criminal elements. They've dabbled in arms transport, but our people think they're pretty sure it's financial services for other bad guys and selected businesses."

"Sounds like common criminal stuff, Charlie. What am I not getting?"

"The Union is an uncommon criminal group. I wish I knew more. I have requested more details from the European authorities, but I'm not receiving much. Our informants are not trusted and thus do not provide a ton of value. I was just going over their paperwork. Nothing significant to move on."

"Let me see," I replied as Charlie handed me a thick multi-tabbed folder with tons of documents inside each folder tab. I thumbed through the pages, scanning each word communicated by the informants, looking for something that could pull it all together for me. Finally, the waitress brought our food, and I began inhaling it. The steak smelled wonderful and was juicy and lean as I cut into it, while the eggs were a perfect sidekick, perfectly cooked with just a little added salt and pepper.

Charlie noted my eating speed and said, "Well, buddy, looks like you were starving."

I smiled with a mouth full of food and pointed at one of the pages in the folder. "Who's this Informant?"

Charlie reached over and flicked the red tab on the folder. "I'm not sure, but he's dead, so he won't be helping us. Red sticker means they are no longer available for questions."

I rolled my eyes. "That's not helping. How about this? Are there *any* unusual comments? You know, bizarre outliers? Things that don't line up with anything? We've got to be missing something here," I said as I continued eating and reading.

Charlie picked up a thinner, manila folder, flipped it through it, "No, I don't.... Wait. Here's a strange quote from Mr. Staple-Toes. I highlighted it to check out, but never found anything. He says he overheard a female during a check-in call. It makes no sense, though."

"What does it say?"

"Quote, 'Sixty tables, the house is blind, the birds are fake, but the fantasies are real.' That's it."

I looked out the window, picking up a thousand-yard stare, then glancing down at my notebook to jot this down, "Sixty tables, the house is blind.... The birds are fake..., but the fantasies are real? That makes no sense."

"That's what it says, Jack. Sounds like part of a conversation, but he only heard her side."

"Could be a coded message. Did Staple-Toes say anything about codes or previous engagements where codes were used? Anything else?"

Charlie flipped through the rest of the pages, then flipped back to the page he had read, "The informant overheard the comments while at Randal's Kitchen, north side of Wellspoint. That's it. Nothing about historic code use. Here, look for yourself."

I took the folder and skimmed through it. "Can you ask Staple-Toes if there's anything else he can remember? Like, who said these words?"

"Okay. I'll do that. Do you recognize the place?" Charlie said.

"I do, good food. Really good coffee."

We synchronously glanced at our own cups of coffee and then back at one another.

"Well, this stuff has given me freakin coffee PTSD," Charlie replied, leaning back away from the table.

"I concur," I replied with raised eyebrows, twisting my head to the side, just a tick of a neck twist. "Charlie, these look like murder cases. Mind if I hold onto these? I'm a decent analyst, ya know."

"Yeah, sure, take them for the weekend. I can't figure them out. At least seven oddball deaths, all related to the appearance and in the vicinity of Miokin or Spake between Wellspoint and Cincinnati. There's got to be a link, but I just can't see it. Like you said, these guys have some help somewhere." Charlie stared at me, eyes narrowing.

I made a few notes in my notebook and then stuffed it back into my pocket.

"That thing is like Indiana Jones' father's notebook: you have a ton of stuff in there," Charlie quipped as he took a drink of horrible coffee. "We have to put a stop to this."

I nodded affirmatively as I thumbed through the files. Then I noticed Charlie's stare.

"What?"

Charlie continued staring at me.

"You are not my Commander anymore, Charlie. What's the problem?"

"With Chief Borland sidelined, you need to rally the team. Make sure you keep everything under control. Don't let Miokin get ahead of you. Keep anything of value out of his reach, especially if it can be used against you or Wellspoint. Help me find out what he's doing there; then we'll take him down."

I shifted in my seat and then sat up straighter, "Oh, I'll find Miokin, and when I do, I'm going to end him—"

"No, Jack. You're a cop. We need to know what they are doing. Don't lose us the war because you are pissed off and want revenge."

I twisted in my booth seat, "You're worried about me? Why'd you let Russell Spake go? We took him off the streets, and you guys put him right back out there. A very capable, freaking bad guy. He probably supervised at least one of these attacks. That was dumb and dangerous, Charlie." I replied.

"I don't have to explain anything. And for the record, these decisions are not mine. The agent in charge at the field office makes those decisions with input from me and the counselor. There's always a bigger picture, Jack."

I received a text message from Oli and stared out the window for a full sixty seconds before responding and setting the phone on the booth's tabletop. I rubbed my eyes with my finger and thumb, then rubbed my face, then I glanced at my watch. Finally, I smiled at Charlie, turned and made the check-signing motion in the air so the waitress could see it. She gave me a thumbs-up. "I gotta go, Charlie. I've got another case to finish. I'll stay in touch. By the way, thanks for sending the code blue."

"Good luck. I'll check in with Staple-Toes and let you know what I find out."

# Chapter 10

My father used to tell my brother and me that changing someone's behavior by force is nearly impossible. You have to make them *want* to do things differently, and that involves incentive, not pain. However, my time in the Army taught me that a combination of taking someone's time and inflicting some pain *is* effective. It was time to test the balance of these theories.

"Can I speak with Jonas Crutchfield?  I was referred to him by a buddy who says he's an expert with 1968 Mustangs," I said to the early-twenties, male clerk.

I'd been in Adrenaline Autos for about twenty minutes, watching the flow of the employees. I was wearing a black Motley Crue t-shirt, a "Horsepower" embroidered baseball cap, and a quarter smile. The place was spacious, brightly lit, with a polished white floor and a dozen rows of automotive supplies on display behind a beige counter that neatly divided the room in half.  A 1967 Chevy Nova, with its hood propped open and a gleaming engine featuring beautifully accented chrome components, was on display in the customer zone. Despite the room's clean appearance, it smelled of oil and rubber from the rows of competition tires stored in racks across the back of the cavernous room and the dull hum of massive overhead air circulating fans chopping through the air.

"Sure," he said and then turned his head and yelled, "J, you've got a customer up front," as he turned and walked away.

Jonas, probably late teens or early twenties, walked up to me with a tablet in one hand and a can of Red Bull in the other. He was about five feet eight inches tall, with a muscular build, long, dark, slicked-back hair, numerous tattoos on his left arm, and a single skull earring in his left ear. He set his can down on the counter. "What can I do for you, chief?"

"I need a performance intake manifold and camshaft for a 1968 Mustang, 302 Windsor engine."

He nodded and started navigating the tablet's interface, laying it on the counter between us, and scrolled to the correct part of the user interface, which displayed Ford intake manifolds.

My cell phone chimed with an apparent inbound message. I took the phone out of my pocket and, after appearing to read the message, I shook my head from side to side. "Man, this woman can be such a nag."

Jonas's eyes raised to meet mine, his face generated a slight grimace, then he chuckled, "I know what you mean. It takes work to keep 'em in line."

I gave a low, short whistle. "Yeah, gotta be careful though," I replied, "had a buddy who put his hands on his girlfriend a little too much; cops came and took him out of his workplace in cuffs, shamed him in front of all his coworkers. I *heard* that when he got outside, he resisted arrest a little too much, and he ended up in jail with a split lip and a gash over his eye." I replied coldly, staring Jonas down with a motionless, penetrating gaze. I watched as Jonas's eyes moved from looking at the stitches over my eye to my swollen, stitched lip. "Spending twenty-four hours in the city jail isn't good for anyone's employment, that much I can tell you. Situations like that can ruin a guy. And honestly, nobody likes that guy, *Nobody*." I said with a shift to a furrowed brow, a quarter smile and a slight nod.

As the weight of my words sank in, Jonas's eyes betrayed him, his pupils constricting in a fleeting moment of vulnerability before blinking a little too fast and then regaining control. Then he replied, with his voice a little hoarse but sufficiently detached to maintain his poise, "Yeah, man, about the Windsor, I've got three matched intake manifolds, camshaft sets. Do you want max horsepower or just a hot rod sound?"

"Can you give me the price for all three? I need to think about it."

He printed out a list and handed it to me, and I unceremoniously turned and walked out to my car and texted Oli. I let him know that I'd met with Sarah's boyfriend, and I think I'd delivered the needed message without letting him know who I was or getting violent. Unfortunately for me, Oli replied that he had a rather unpleasant update for me, so I needed to get over to ByteStep Computers ASAP.

* * *

"What do you mean, Oli? I already closed the damned case based on the report in your email," I said with my hands on my hips in the reception area of ByteStep Computing, standing across the counter from Oli.

"I'm sorry, Jack; this was a late-breaking find; it seriously changes things." Oil replied, "Come to the back; let me show you what I'm talking about."

We walked to the rear of ByteStep, into a small, bright conference room where Sarah was connecting her laptop to a larger screen at the end of the rectangular, eight-seat table. I could hear the rush of dry, crisp-smelling air pressing through vents at one end of the room, and the table had a small island in the center that hosted several wires and cables, apparently for connecting to the room's video and audio displays. Along one length of the room was a countertop with plain metal stools. There were several gadgets, specialized-looking instruments on top of the counter that I recognized as computer forensics tools. The room had a laboratory vibe to it.

"Oli, I've already emailed the report to the deputy mayor. The mayor is going to mention that the investigation has concluded in an hour over at the freakin university!"

Oli gave me a flat, two-handed downward gesture, lowering both hands. "Please sit, Jack. This is important." Oli said.

So we all sat.

I leaned back in my chair with my arms folded as Sarah began describing the data anomaly affecting log events around the time the deceased was overtaken. "When I analyzed the log events, I mostly looked at the meaning of the events, but this morning I thought something was odd about the events themselves. The sequencing during that critical period of time, in particular, as compared to previous logs. It took some time, but I managed to develop a program that accurately measures the distribution, variance, and entropy of inter-event times. The deltas,"

I looked at Oli with a furrowed brow. "Just wait a sec, Jack, this is good," he said.

Sarah scooted forward in her seat just an inch before continuing, "Here, see the date and time events from these three systems?" She highlighted tabular data events on the screen from three categories: the $CO_2$ storage tank array controller, as there are twelve cylinders, the fire suppression system controller, and the $CO_2$ gas detector controller. "All three systems' event logs from 6:01 a.m. to 12:01 p.m. are too perfectly distributed. Here, see, when the logs are aggregated together, the standard deviation of the log date times is very low with very low measured entropy. I think this means that someone generated these logs together, then split them, feeding them back into each system individually, so the log collectors would aggregate them back into their SIEM, making them appear normal when separately analyzed by SOC personnel. When evaluated together, there's no mistaking the manipulated date-times of the logs."

"So taken individually, like, logs from the $CO_2$ storage tank array controller, analysis of them looks normal? The distribution is okay?" I replied.

"That's right, detective," Sarah said. "It's only when you compare all the data as a set that the deception becomes clear. It's like someone meticulously crafted a fake history for each system."

I twisted in my seat, leaning forward, rubbed my chin, turned to look at Oli with narrowing eyes, "Somebody put a lot of technical effort into this." My mind immediately raced to those with access and capability. Daniel Rogers, the student who claimed to be a cybersecurity expert, was the one I'd interviewed at the university, or Sage, in the University's SOC Chief. Daniel and Sage were both quick to say, "There's nothing to see here, detective, please move along."

Oli jumped in, "The troubling thing is, I looked at the data on these disks, and the zipped archive files containing the log files are perfect. Each zipped file has the correct sequential date and times, and the file ordering and file metadata are all just right. Zipped together perfectly in tarred archives. Whoever did this is a damn pro. I'm just glad that Sarah took a second look."

"Do we know what logs could be missing, or if the content of these logs was modified?" I asked with my eyes darting between Oli and Sarah.

"No way," Oli replied, "Jack, this means somebody completely manipulated all log events from those three systems at least during that time frame. All these logs could be complete nonsense or just manipulated dates. Given what we know, it's impossible to derive that without more evidence. The date times on all the other logs from all the other twelve systems seem to check out fine."

I sat back in my seat, considering this new bit of evidence. "Well, *shit.* I'm going to have to go back over to the University SOC. Okay, any recommended next steps?" I asked.

Oli considered my words and rubbed his own stubble-filled chin. "Yes. You should investigate and determine who had access to those three systems. Full access to the file systems and the log aggregators. Then get your hands on their SEIM backup snapshots. There's a chance those archived logs are not manipulated, but I wouldn't put anything past whoever did this. They likely thought of everything. There could be something outside their reach, though. Something they cannot easily get to, or something they missed."

"How do I do that? Some of those systems are no longer online."

Oli smiled broadly, leaning back in his seat. He put both hands behind his head, leaning back in a fake stretching motion. *Ever the presenter that Oli.* Then, in a single, human hand grenade burst of extroversion, his right hand broke free from the back of his head, and he pointed at Sarah over and over again. "Well, that's easy, Jackie, my boy. Let me bring you into Oli's world of how to get stuff done in the wonderful world of tech! You are going to take Sarah Becker here with you to the university. Act pissed off, and tell them that she's going to take some unannounced forensic samples of a few systems. I'll give Sarah one of our collection kits, and we'll see what we can see. You are going to be 'Pissed Off' because someone lied to you or faked some logs or something. Put everyone on notice that you, Detective Jack Stewart, are not going to be screwed with!"

Oli stood up and made some bodybuilder-style muscle poses, first showing his nonexistent biceps, then leaning over to reveal his nonexistent trapezius muscles. Sarah shifted in her seat, eyes opening wide and leaning into the conversation.

The room fell quiet as my eyes moved between Oli and Sarah a few times. "I don't know Oli, if there is a killer out there, I don't want them coming after Sarah. Also, that's a lot of pressure—"

Sarah stood abruptly, placing her hands on the table and leaning into it, "Oh please, I can do this, detective. This is perfect; it's exactly what I am here to do! Please, I can do it. I'll help you catch the murderer!" she said with a high-pitched, squeaky voice and eyes a mile wide.

"I can't go, Jack. I have to be at the courthouse in an hour, and I need to prepare for that testimony. You have one shot to get something useful by catching them off guard. You also need to get your asses moving if you're going to prevent the mayor from making a Grade-A liar out of himself on the university's stage."

I lowered my head and began rubbing my temples. *Well shit. I'm officially stuck. Maybe this is how Chief Borland feels when I badger him with my crazy schemes to catch bad guys*, I thought. "Okay, hold on a sec. If we were going to do this, how should we approach it?" I asked Oli.

Oli leaned forward, looked at Sarah, "Sarah, we've trained you for this. Go get one of the laptops with the multi-interface kits and your jacket." Oli turned to look at me, "Here's how to do this. You've got to play it just right because if you don't, they can block you just by asking for a subpoena. Do they have security in that building?"

"Yeah, there's an older guy there that hands out badges, that sort of thing, I think I can get him to help," I replied, smiling with a wolfish, predatory grin.

"Perfect, you handle the guard," Oli said. Oli gave me a lot of helpful recommendations, and we discussed the pitfalls to avoid. Sarah came back into the room with a black hooded sweatshirt on that read "Bytes My Ass" across the front. Reading that, I glanced down at a now-seated Oli, giving him the side-eye, and he said, "Relax, Jack, this will be noooo problem."

I thought about her huge, angry father, Becker, and how he would try to dismember me if he ever found out about this little endeavor.

Still standing, I continued giving Oli the side eye, then looked at Sarah with a half-smile, exhaling heavily through my nose. "Okay, let's go;

we've got to beat the mayor's speech or all of this falls apart."

The three of us walked out the front door and down the steps. Oli looked at me, patting me on the back with his left hand and said, "This will be a piece of cake, Jack. Sarah gets experience; you catch the bad guys; ByteStep computers helps you solve the case, on the cheap, I might add. I mean, you are not paying for the field collection work. Anyway, everyone wins, except the bad guys of course," Oli was beaming, "We've got noooo problems—"

Walking toward us up the sidewalk was none other than Sarah's boyfriend, Jonas Crutchfield. He walked up to us and froze when he saw me. I was still wearing the black Motley Crue T-shirt and jeans but not the hat. Sarah ran up to him. His eyes darted between Sarah and me, and he said that he would wait for her later at their hangout if she still intended to meet. She was very excited and told him she'd be there but late, as she had to go on a "special mission." He wished her luck, gave her a careful, side hug, and then turned and walked away, glancing at Oli and me twice before picking up a full cadence.

Oli and I exchanged glances. I dropped my shoulders just an inch, exhaling as Oli looked at me thoughtfully and said through gritted teeth. "Okay, we've got ooone problem!"

Ten minutes later, on the way back to the University, Sarah asked a question that stumped me. "Do you think the murderer will be at the event tonight?" I glanced between the road and Sarah twice, considering the potential depth of that question.

I looked at her with a furrowed brow that transitioned downwards into a guarded smile, "It's possible." I shrugged, "I've caught lesser criminals who executed smartly. We both need to have an extra eye out, looking for someone who could be surveilling us."

Sarah peered out the window, probably thinking about how she'd proceed when we arrived. *She's exceptionally thoughtful*, I considered.

I raised my badge high in my left hand as we boldly walked through the SOC doors at the University, "Attention, I'm Detective Jack Stewart, and I'm here to collect additional data in support of an investigation." The security guard was standing next to me, sweating profusely from the walk up the stairs and the stress of my not listening very well to his directions to badge in or call Dr. Davies prior to entering the facility.

"This is Ms. Sarah B. She'll be facilitating the forensics data collection. Please do not obstruct her," I said, looking right at Sage, holding up my folded dry cleaning bill in my right hand for a moment, then placing it back into my pocket.

The security guard spoke, "It's okay, folks, I've notified Dr. Davies and the University security chief; please do as Detective Stewart asks."

Sage approached from the main desk. She looked at Sarah carefully, then at me with a slight tilt to her head. "Hello, Sage. This is Sarah. If you'll help her get access to the data she's looking for, that would be great."

Sage looked at Sarah and offered her a handshake, "I'm Sage, the SOC director here at the University. It's nice to meet you, Sarah."

Sarah shook her hand, then turned to look at me with a stern, serious look on her face, "Thank you, detective. I'll take it from here." She said it in a voice an octave lower than her normal voice. Sarah turned her back on me and began walking toward Sage's workstation, with Sage taking the lead along the way.

I watched Sarah connect her system to Sage's terminal. Sarah glanced at me once, then again.

"I turned to look at the security guard. "Okay, looks like you have things under control here, Sergeant. I'll be back. I need to track down another lead," I said, giving him a solid slap on the shoulder, then spinning to bolt out of the room before he could respond.

# Chapter 11

"What the hell is wrong with you, detective?" the deputy mayor said, grabbing me by the elbow and whisking me into a backstage, side room of the auditorium.  I noticed he walked like a penguin.  *How odd*, I thought. I let him drag me away from the crowded lobby. Then, just to reinforce that I'm six feet four inches and weigh 195 pounds, I decided to stop in my tracks. He lost his grip and took the last two steps into the backstage, side room without me.

Once in the side room, I strode independently toward the curtain's edge just out of sight from the massive student and local audience. I noted the mayor, Dr. Davies, a city councilwoman I recognized, and a male in his late forties who seemed vaguely familiar.  They were all seated at the table, each behind a microphone, with a moderator I didn't recognize standing twenty feet away at a podium. The backstage auditorium was pitch dark, smelled like mothballs and ozone as the bright lights above pounded everyone on or near the stage with old-fashioned heat and intense light, giving a bit of a magic show vibe.

"Detective!" the deputy mayor said, trying to recapture my attention.

I turned to look at him with my hands raised slightly and a furrowed brow, "Sir, I had to reopen the case because recent evidence indicated foul play in the death of Brett Savoy. There's something going on that we've got to sort out."

The deputy mayor glared at me. "What is the nature of this *recent evidence*, detective?" he asked with derision, contorting his face.

"Well, sir, it's complicated, but the bottom line is someone manipulated log events from three key subsystems that were associated with the $CO_2$ arresting system at the time of the incident. Those specific subsystems allegedly failed, causing Brett Savoy's death."

"Okay, meaning what then?"

"Well, what it means is someone had access to those systems, and they changed or manipulated the logs at precisely the victim's time of death, probably to avoid detection."

The deputy mayor put his hands on his hips and whispered, "You overgrown baboon, why couldn't you have texted me this hour ago? The mayor has mentioned the case is closed twice already. *The case is supposed to be closed.* Dr. Davies and Dr. Turner have already highlighted how they're moving forward now that *the case is closed.*"

Options reeled through my mind as I peered at the deputy mayor blankly. Finally, I made my decision. "Don't worry, sir, I won't tell him you screwed this up." I gave him a solid pat on the back with my long-reaching left arm, causing him to wince as I spun around and walked out onto the stage. I received a lot of stares from the audience and the panel members. I walked over to the mayor and got down onto one knee, whispering in his ear. He jerked his head back to look at me thoroughly with raised eyebrows and an open mouth. Then he turned to look at the deputy mayor, still standing over in the off-stage area.

The man standing at the podium tried to regain control of the situation, saying, "Excuse me, sir, can I help you? We're in the middle of a panel; it would be great if you could get off stage for now. You can get the mayor's autograph after the session."

The mayor reached down to turn his microphone on and looked down at the other panelists, then turned his head back toward the audience. "It seems we may have been premature with our decision to close the case, so Detective Stewart here is telling me that the case is still open, and we have a few more corners to close before it will be fully resolved. I think it will be accomplished in short order."

The audience reacted with lots of side conversations as several journalists in the front row strained their arms, trying to get the moderator's attention for a question.

I walked back into the off-stage area, and the deputy mayor glared at me, saying, "You did that just to embarrass me, didn't you?"

I replied, "Look, sir, I'm just trying to do my job here and do it well. That's what I do, solve problems, catch the bad guys, and I have a pretty good record of doing that in case you didn't notice."

The deputy mayor gritted his teeth and whispered, "I'm going to get you for this, you imbecile. You need to learn how things work around here."

The mayor expertly handled the explosion of audience questions before the moderator mercifully ended the event. As the event closed, I could hear the murmurs of numerous audience members chatting with one another, like bees buzzing about a bed of flowers. Four or five journalists pressed forward to the edge of the stage, shouting questions at Dr. Davies and the mayor.

The mayor, the man I vaguely recognized, and Dr. Davies made a beeline for me and the red-faced deputy mayor. The mayor was a regal figure, a tall man about my height with salt-and-pepper hair, a strong chin, and an intimidating set of green eyes set deeply in his sockets. The gentleman I didn't know introduced himself, saying, "Hello, detective. My name is Dr. Ira Turner. I have a few questions—"

Dr. Davies immediately joined the conversation, asking, "Detective, could you please describe the new evidence and explain how you interpreted it?

I replied, forcing a smile that didn't quite make it to my eyes, "Hello, Dr. Davies. We completed the analysis of the cybersecurity event logs from the SOC. We determined that logs from three of your systems were heavily modified, indicating someone changed them around the time Brett Savoy was killed."

Dr. Turner's face shifted to a pained look, his mouth closed, and his eyes drooped, glancing toward the floor.

My cell phone rang, and I saw it was a call from Sarah. So I stepped away from the group, saying, "Excuse me one moment, please. This is an important call."

As I returned to the group and smiled, I heard Dr. Davies say one word to the mayor: "... *Incompetent.*"

"Dr. Turner, it was very nice to meet you. I think I recognize your name; you are Brett's Professor, right?"

That's right," he said. "Brett was a wonderful student and had such a bright future, it's very unfortunate how that situation turned out."

"Yes, indeed. Can you tell me if Jasmine Garcia or Christina was involved with Brett? Did they spend time with him?"

The professor cocked his head to the side and said, "Detective, I'm not sure we have a common frame of reference, but I don't know much about Brent's friends and associates beyond the University. He spent a lot of time with Luna Ross. He worked on the Computerized Hyperadaptive Realtime Intelligence for Security, Transactions, Insight, Networks, and Automation. Many students do."

Something clicked in my head. That was a mouthful and would make for quite an acronym. The students build the computers, and they likely name them. *If the Union is aware of this computer, that would explain a few things.*

"Computerized Hyperadaptive Realtime Intelligence for Security, Transactions, Insight, Networks, and Automation? There's got to be a more succinct way to say that. Christina?" I asked.

"Yes, that's right; it's a sophisticated automation and security platform, based on our university's custom decision engine."

"Decision engine, okay, that makes sense," I said as I pulled out my notebook and jotted down a quick note. "Do you recall Brent being accompanied by a tall blond woman? Maybe in class or around the campus. You'd likely remember, very statuesque and pretty with waist-length platinum blond hair?"

His eyebrows raised, and he looked across the room, then back to me, "No, detective, I'm sorry; I don't recall anyone like that."

The mayor rejoined the group after spending some time answering questions from the press.

"Detective Stewart, I'd like you and a guest to join us tonight here at the university ballroom. The city is sponsoring a dinner to celebrate computer science achievements," he said.

Dr. Davies' jaw dropped as she looked between the mayor and me.

"Thank you, sir, but—"

"I understand it's a last-minute engagement, but I think police presence will assist with optics here at the university. Please, I insist," he said with his eyebrows lowered, casting a shadow over his eyes.

"Okay, no problem, sir; I'd be honored to attend," I said, standing up straighter.

"Great, I'll have Brian send you the details. See you at seven then," the mayor said, extending his right hand for a shake.

*So I shook it.*

With that, he turned and left with his publicist and assistant in tow, just as the deputy mayor filled the space the mayor vacated in our circular discussion group.

My phone chimed with a text message from Sarah, which I read by peeking at my watch: "I need help!"

I glanced between the deputy mayor and Dr. Davies, "Okay, well, I have to head back over to the Cook Center to pick up the new batch of forensics data your team facilitated. Sincerely appreciate the help from security. Sorry to rain on the panel event."

I turned and walked briskly up the auditorium walkway.

* * *

The air inside the Cooke Center lobby felt thick, charged with a silent, brewing situation. When I returned, the usual polite hum of activity had been replaced by a brittle stillness. Sarah Becker stood locked in a tense standoff with a young security officer, his grip tight on the strap of her backpack. The officer's older counterpart hovered nearby, a silent observer to the unfolding drama.

"You can't take my forensics evidence!" Sarah's voice, though controlled, held a raw edge of defiance. *She's in a tough spot*, I thought, *let's give her a hand.*

I walked toward them, the knot in my stomach from dealing with the mayor twisting with each step. Flashing my badge, I forced a smile, hoping to diffuse the situation before it escalated. "Whoa, everybody just take a breath here."

I stepped within twelve inches of the young security guard, looking down at him. He was approximately five feet eight inches tall, weighing around 130 pounds. He wisely stepped backwards a half step but held onto the bag.

"I think you're doing an admirable job, Ted," I said, looking at his nameplate and smiling at his silent partner. "I was just with Dr. Davies and Dr. Turner; they understand what's occurred. Please take up any issues with them." I grabbed the bag and, with a single powerful upward motion, I swiftly ripped it out of his hands and handed it to Sarah.

I turned and looked at Sarah. Her jaw was clenched, and her eyes were narrowed as she glared at Ted. "Okay," I said. "Come on, Miss Becker. Time to go."

When we got to the edge of the lobby, Dr. Davies walked in with Dr. Turner. She stopped me and said, "I'd like to have a follow-up conversation with you, detective. I was talking with Dr. Turner, and I would like to understand the nature of these anomalies better."

I turned to look at Sarah and said, "Go ahead, give them the lowdown." They both looked at Sarah and her sweatshirt. Glancing at each other, I looked back at Sarah as she explained the anomaly she'd detected.

"I'm sorry, who do you work for? What are your credentials?" Dr. Davies asked Sarah with a forced smile.

"My name is Sarah Becker, and I'm a computer forensics analyst. I work for ByteStep Computers," she said proudly as she noted Dr. Davies taking in the "Bytes My Ass" slogan across the front of her hooded sweatshirt before breaking into a full smile.

I broke in, "Okay, we have to go; there is a lot of evidence to go through here. We're leaving. I will circle back with both of you tomorrow with an update."

"Will we see you tonight, detective?" Dr. Turner asked in earnest.

I stood upright, smiling at them both and replied, "Yes, I'll be there at seven. Likely alone on such short notice."

"Why don't you bring Ms. Becker here?" replied Dr. Davies.

I smiled again, "That's an interesting idea, thank you, Dr. Davies. If you'll please excuse us, we need to get going."

Sarah and I walked briskly to the car, and I glanced at her a couple of times. She had that thousand-yard stare, like someone replaying how they would have liked to have responded in a situation.

"You okay?" I asked her on the way back to ByteStep Computers.

She looked at me, then back toward the road and said, "Yes, I'm okay, just was not anticipating all the friction and—"

"And, opinionated discussion?" I replied, finishing an octave higher than normal.

A smile burst onto Sarah's face as she glanced at me before returning to look at the road ahead.

I smiled, my eyes crinkling at the corners, and I looked at her for a couple of seconds before migrating my eyes back to the road.

It got quiet again for a minute or two.

"What was your impression of Sage? Do you think she's part of it?" I asked Sarah.

"I can't tell for sure," she said, "but I don't think so. I think she's worried about one of her employees, though. Someone who's going through some trouble."

We sat quietly as we approached the Starbucks near ByteStep computers, where Oli and I often met.

"I think it's time for coffee, Sarah."

"Coffee?" she quarter-smiled. "I don't drink coffee, I mean, not really."

"Well, when you're hunting for murderers," I said, "it's important to stop and drink something. Cops drink coffee. Maybe forensics engineers drink soda or tea?"

She smiled, looking back toward the road. "Tea works."

"Great, we all need to try a variety of things in life to help drive the best possible decisions," I replied using a British accent with a touch of wry humor in my voice.

Sarah giggled then replied with her own British-accented comment, "A spot of tea does seem in order."

* * *

"Well, how did it go?" Oli asked as we strolled back into ByteStep Computers' conference room, his broad smile plastered widely onto his face.

We all sat down at the conference table, and Sarah opened her laptop to review the data.

"It went well," I replied, "Sarah did a fantastic job. We managed to get a ton of data, so all is well."

Sarah's eyes darted between Oli and me, asking, "Do you think I can join you tonight at the university?"

I glanced at Ollie, who raised an eyebrow before turning back to me. "What is this?" he asked with an elevated pitch in his voice.

"Well, we got the message to the mayor a little late," I explained, "so he'd already closed the case during a public panel. I let him know about the anomalies."

"Okay? So how did that work?" Oli replied, his brow furrowed in concern.

"Well, it didn't go smoothly, but I just walked out onto the stage and told him I had to reopen the case. Ticked off the deputy mayor, of course. They ended up finishing the panel early, and the mayor did a Q&A session with the local media. Apparently, they conveyed concerns for the safety of the students and the locals."

"You walked out onto the stage during the panel event?" Oli asked, chuckling nervously.

"Yes, I did, Oli," I replied through gritted teeth. "I didn't have much choice. Bad news never gets better with age; it only gets worse." The memory of the flashbulbs and the echoing questions felt fresh, a phantom pressure on my chest.

Sarah jumped in, her voice laced with a forced cheerfulness. "So the mayor thought it would be good for Detective Stewart to make an appearance at the event tonight. Showing local law enforcement support."

"The idea grated on me, but it did seem like a way to get some questions answered," I replied, looking between Oli and Sarah. I paused, looking across the room at the door, considering how this could backfire. Finally, I nodded, the movement was tight. "Yep. It was a late notice invitation, so I mentioned I'd likely attend alone, and Dr. Davies thought it would be great if Sarah joined us. I think that might be a bit too risky, though." The thought of her, bright and observant, being a target sent a wave of anxiety through me.

Sarah's face fell. The color drained from her cheeks, and she looked genuinely wounded, like she'd been punched in the gut. Her silence was louder than any outburst.

"Why not?" Oli asked, his tone softening, sensing the tension.

"It's late," I said, struggling to keep my voice level. "I don't want to get her too involved. I don't want any trouble, and I don't want a... murderer like Miokin coming after her." The name hung in the air, a palpable threat. Miokin was a determined and dangerous criminal, a dark shadow that had immediate reach in Wellspoint of late.

Sarah stood, looked between Oli and me like she was about to scream, then she stormed out, the door clicking shut with a finality that felt unsettling.

Oli broke the silence, a nervous chuckle escaping him. "Okay, well, it is an interesting opportunity for her to hang out with, you know, computer nerds."

"Damn it, Oli! I don't want a murderer coming after her! And then there's Becker. I feel like he'd go to great lengths to beat me, ruin me, and torture me, and not in that order. The guy's level of hate for the cop that beat and then arrested his son is off the damned chart!" I yelled, the frustration boiling over.

We sat quietly for a few minutes, the weight of the situation pressing down on us. Then, Sarah came back into the room, clutching a bottle of water like a lifeline. She sat back down, but only sat at the edge of her seat, a coiled spring, radiating nervous energy.

Oli shifted in his seat, glanced at Sarah and then back at me. "Jack, it will probably be a twoish-hour event. I think she'll be okay. Just stay close to her and, you know...."

I looked at Oli, cocked my head, and said through gritted teeth. "You know... *what?*"

"Keep an eye on her: keep her near the table, away from people, and leave as soon as the session starts winding down. There's no need to be there for the entire event. I doubt anyone will even notice her."

Sarah stood and started slowly pacing, her agitation palpable. Then she sat down at the table. "That's right, I'll dress like all the other students and try to blend in. You won't even know I'm there, detective." Her voice held a determined edge.

We sat quietly, me glancing between Sarah and Oli, then staring at the floor. The pattern of the carpet seemed to swirl before my eyes.

It occurred to me that this was the second time today I'd been officially stuck: a pawn in someone else's game.

"Sarah, if we do this, you're going to have to be very careful about what you say and who you say it to. We have to be very careful in this situation."

Sarah's eyes sparkled with fierce excitement, a spark of defiance. "I won't let you down, detective. This is perfect! I'll be back in twenty minutes. I'm going to change clothes."

And with that, she bolted out the door, leaving Oli and me looking at each other in a mixture of concern and amusement.

Oli suddenly stood up and clapped his hands together, rubbing them in a warming motion. "Well, at least she won't be hanging out with her boyfriend tonight," he smirked, trying to lighten the mood.

I gave him the side eye, and with a wry grin, I replied in a near whisper, "Thank you, that's very helpful, Oli."

# Chapter 12

I thought my fly was down.

Everyone stared at us as we walked slowly to our table across the student hall. There were four rows of round, ten-person tables, each filled with moderately dressed students, faculty, and locals, all enjoying the provided dinner. The room had a high ceiling, bright lighting, and the air carried a citrusy scent, giving a super-clean conference room vibe as a technician worked on the podium's audio system on the rectangular stage near the front of the room.

"Welcome, detective, we've got you two seated over here by the mayor and Dr. Davies," said the brightly-dressed student greeter as she motioned for us to follow her. She strolled, smiling to acquaintances as we took a circuitous route to our table.

"Thank you, looks like everyone is already eating; I suppose we are late then?" I said, trying to recall the schedule.

The social was from 5:30 to 6:30, and dinner started at 6:30 p.m. The presentations are about to start, so you are on time for the show," she replied.

Sarah placed her beige blazer over the back of her seat; her pants were black, and her skinny but well-defined arms stretched through her bright, sleeveless button-down shirt. She smiled at Dr. Davies. She pulled the chair into a position she liked, then sat down. I remained standing, making eye contact with each of the guests at the table as the student greeter performed introductions.

"This is Dr. Ji Won Kim, Dr. Davies, Dr. Turner, Malachi Hunter, Ginger Rowland, and I think you know the mayor, his wife Lucia, and the deputy mayor and his wife, Jeanne," the student said. My eyes followed the introductions until I stopped cold, eyes widening, immediately stuck on Ginger, who was sitting next to a slender, dark-haired man. Ginger's emerald-green eyes seemed especially bold in the ambient green of her bright earrings and deep green blazer. Her brown hair was freshly trimmed just below her shoulders, and, even in a half-smile, she was captivating. She sat very still, her eyes darting around the table and back to me.

The mayor smiled at Sarah and me and said, "Welcome, detective. Please have a seat, we're about to get started."

Ginger blinked fast, looking between the mayor and me and glancing toward Malachi Hunter.

Malachi put down his napkin and stood, reaching across the table, "It's nice to meet you, detective. Ginger has told me so much about you."

Sarah nudged me after a few seconds. I glanced at her and then sat down and shook his hand, being careful not to reach over anyone. "Mr. Hunter, it's nice to meet you as well. Ginger, it's... great to see you," I said with a full-on grin and deadpan voice.

We started eating as sidebars broke out in a low hum across the room.

"Someone you know?" whispered Sarah.

"Yes, my ex," I whispered back.

I glanced at Ji Won; her gaze met mine as I nodded once and smiled warmly. Her response was a subtle nod, accompanied by that stunningly beautiful smile, "Detective Stewart, it's good to see you joining us this evening."

I glanced back at Ginger to see her giving me a quarter side eye as she pretended to be engaged in the conversation between Malachi and Dr. Turner.

Sarah was chatting away with Dr. Davies, who was wearing a grey jumpsuit and an interested expression, while Dr. Turner, in a dark blue blazer and white business shirt, sat to her right, engaged with Malachi. I shifted to focus on the mayor. "Sir, thank you again for the invitation; this is fantastic."

"Yes, detective, this is a wonderful facility. The city has made a lot of investments here to grow the next generation," the mayor said as we entered chit-chat mode.

The deputy mayor, wearing a grey shirt, a tightly tied blue tie, and a checkered blazer, was sitting to my left and leaned over, whispering in my ear, "Seriously, detective? You're wearing a Motley Crew T-shirt to an official city event?"

I considered his comment and then turned back to look at Ginger for a moment. She was staring at me with her right eyebrow raised and the corners of her mouth turned up ever so slightly. I turned back to the deputy mayor and said, "Sorry, it's been a busy day. I *am* wearing a jacket, and most importantly, I'm not wearing stinky basketball shoes," I chuckled.

The deputy mayor glared at me and, with mock sincerity, replied, "That's terrific, detective, I suppose we should all be grateful you are wearing shoes."

I noticed Dr. Turner got up to get drinks at the bar, so I followed him.

"This is quite the facility, Dr. Turner. It looks like you could play football in here." I said, smiling.

He smiled back and replied, "This facility is only four years old; it's in its prime, and we use it for a variety of functions thanks to its digital versatility."

The crowd fell silent as the lights dimmed and the ceremony began. In the distance, I could see Sarah standing next to Ginger, leaning over, looking at Ginger's cell phone.

"Well, it looks like they're rolling out the red carpet for this Malachi Hunter fellow," I said.

"Yes, detective, Malachi is a *big* donor," he replied.

We both paused to clap as Malachi received an award from the mayor and Dr. Davies for his financial contributions to the university's computer science program.

"Dr. Turner, we talked earlier about Christina. Could you help me understand a bit more about her?" I asked.

"Oh, yes, detective," Dr. Turner said. "It's a crowning achievement."

"Fantastic," I said as we inched a few feet further in line, "Please continue."

"Christina is a special platform that is trained to perform cybersecurity and similar tasks for very large independent systems," Dr. Turner explained. "It's world-class artificial intelligence, in a production environment."

"Okay, I get it," I said, raising my eyebrows. "Christina is not a person, it's a computer."

Dr. Turner chuckled. "Yes, very much so, albeit an elaborate computer of immense computational capability."

"Great," I said. "So, is it used to protect the networks at the university?"

"Oh no," Dr. Turner replied. "We have a system, an earlier prototype of Christina, that performs security and related functions for the university. That is a far less complex suite of tasks, by the way."

"Interesting," I said. "Where is Christina then?"

"Well, I'll give you *some* details, but the details are NDA'd due to sensitivities with the customer."

"The customer?" I asked.

"Yes, detective," Dr. Turner said. "You see, we research and build sophisticated technologies here at the university, and one of the ways we sustain ourselves is by selling the research or technologies to businesses and other organizations. In many cases, our intellectual property is sold or licensed for large sums of money. However, in this case, there's only one customer for Christina."

"Okay," I said with a broad smile, "I'm interested. Who's the customer?"

"Detective," Dr. Turner said, "I'll have to ask you to sign a nondisclosure agreement. Are you willing to do that?"

"Sure, no problem," I replied.

"Okay," he said. "We can do that tomorrow. But for now, I'll tell you that Christina is the heart and soul of the Fantasy Casino, downtown."

I furrowed my brow, trying to put the pieces together as I kept my smile going, nodding my head up and down. "Yes, that place looks complicated, and I could see where folks walking around with a bunch of wireless devices could be a security nightmare," I said.

"Yes, the Sparrows. It's quite the sophisticated setup, hundreds of millions of transactions per week." Dr. Turner picked up the two drinks he'd just purchased and said, "Detective, why don't you stop by tomorrow morning, and I'll give you the background needed to understand Christina a little better? A bright smile fluttered across his face."

I picked up my beer and a Coke Zero for Sarah and said, "Yes, good point; we should get back and congratulate Malachi with the rest of the room." I smiled sardonically.

Oli turned out to be right, it was really a short evening. The mayor handed out a few awards, and Dr. Davies presented a few awards while highlighting the achievements of numerous students in the computer science department, which, surprisingly, seemed sophisticated from my uneducated perspective.

I stood near the table, talking with Sarah about the situation. Sarah saw Ginger approaching and commented, "Your Ex is very pretty. How long were you together?"

"Yes, she's a stunner for sure. We've been on and off for about two years. We started getting serious then... well, you know how relationships can be. What's your take?"

"I don't know; she seems quiet, absorbing all the conversations going on—"

Noticing Ginger inbound, I said, "Hang on a second," as I stepped over to intercept Ginger returning from the ladies' room.

"Everything Okay? It's been a while. I need to talk with you." I said quietly.

"What about?"

"Well, you, and are you okay after the situation earlier this week? How did that happen?"

Her eyes met mine, and a slow, deliberate connection occurred. An entire landscape of unspoken thoughts streamed from her eyes to mine. My brain turned into a hurricane where clear thoughts and perspective smashed into a vortex of emotions. I couldn't think of what to say.

"Jack, I just need something new, please don't make a scene."

"Okay, okay, I'm not freaking out or anything, I'm just trying to understand what the heck is going on,"

"We aren't together. I'm dating Malachi. That's all there is for now."

"Okay."

"I need space that isn't constantly overshadowed by your work and the people you deal with, the criminals, the violence; it brings out a monster in you."

"So this is about my job?"

"No, I'm returning to the table, please, Jack."

I swallowed hard and tried to put order to the myriad of thoughts storming through my head. I was frozen in thought. I didn't realize Sarah was still standing nearby, probably trying to determine if I was okay. The roar of audience applause snapped me out of my funk. I smiled at Sarah and said, "We should sit back down." So we short-stepped our way back to the table.

More clapping ensued as the awards portion of the evening appeared to wind down.

A photographer from the Wellspoint Gazette stopped by the table to take pictures of the mayor, who stood to propose a toast, which was well received as it closed the night's events. I raised my glass, trying not to look at Ginger.

* * *

I was deep in thought as I drove Sarah back to ByteStep Computers. Along the way, she asked a couple of interesting questions, especially asking about the elephant in the car.

"That discussion you had with your Ex, well, she seemed to get really... agitated."

I looked over at her and pushed out a fake smile. "I was trying to find out why she was involved in something serious. Not really as focused on us, but I think that's where she went. Was it that obvious?"

She glanced at me and then back toward the road, saying, "Your *discussion* drew a lot of attention. Everyone at the table must have noticed, including her friend." Sarah's words hung innocently in the car as another car passed us.

"I sense a recommendation in there somewhere," I replied with a glance.

"Well, it might be best to focus on what she is really... focused... on," Sarah replied.

I considered her thoughts, *yep, she was right.* "Good idea. I'll do that." I said with a genuine smile as I rubbed the top of my head with my left hand, realizing the true genius of her comment.

Thirty seconds went by

"I noticed you talking with her quite a bit."

Sarah nodded. "She gave me some interesting background, and you know, details. She talked a lot about Mr. Hunter."

"What did you make of Hunter?" I said.

"He seemed to have good business sense... and he seemed calm and collected," she smiled, considering for a moment. "Something was charming about him, I guess," she smiled.

I glanced over at Sarah and then back to the road. "Did you learn anything from Dr. Davies or Dr. Turner that could be helpful?" I asked.

"Yes," Sarah replied. "I got a ton from those conversations; they are really committed to the college. They are very worried about the case being reopened. I did some looking up on my phone, and Dr. Davies is a *Titan* in the field of computer science. There's not as much out there about Dr. Turner from what I could see. He worked at some large companies in the past, but I'm not sure what led him to pursue a university role. I'm guessing he made a lot of money around the programs he was associated with."

"Okay, interesting," I said as I considered her thoughts.

A few quiet minutes passed, and I pulled into ByteStep's parking lot. "Well, this has been great, Sarah. I know this was a long day, but I really appreciate your help." I parked behind her car at the ByteStep parking lot. "I'll wait till you get in your car."

Sarah turned and looked at me, smiling, and said, "It seems to me your ex still likes you."

I exhaled through my nose, rocking back, then breaking into a full smile, and said, "Thanks. You're very perceptive. I got the same feeling."

"Oh, and ah, just a recommendation, I'd consider retiring that shirt. It's a little—," she paused, crinkling the corners of her eyes as though she was in pain, "janky. I'll talk to you tomorrow, detective," Sarah said.

"Okay," I replied as the door shut. *Good tip*, I thought.

As Sarah drove away, my phone chimed with a text message from Ji Won. "Interested in some help? I'm in Building 206 at the end of the street, in the Cooke Center on Marshall Hall. Second floor, room two."

I considered her message and finally replied, typing a short but direct acceptance of her invitation.

# Chapter 13

The fluorescent lights in Ji Won's university office hummed a low, steady drone, while a faint whisp of floral-smelling perfume permeated the area. The clicks of her mechanical keyboard seemed to boom across the quiet room. I hunched over a stack of emails, science department reports, and other related documents, my brow furrowed in concentration. Dr. Turner was quite a prolific businessman. The weight of the case was pressing down on me, while the presence of Ji Won was a welcome distraction.

She stood and stepped over to my table, her dark hair pulled back, the soft glow of the office lights highlighting the intelligence in her eyes. "No luck on event correlation or signs of foul play?" Ji Won asked, her voice a low murmur that carried over the ambient noise.

A weary smile grew across my lips and eyes. "Something like that. This data is tough to interpret. There are so many transactions and technical exchanges, it's hard to see any patterns, let alone a malicious correlation of some kind."

"In graph analytics, the beauty is in the patterns. The frustration is in the unexpected loops." She gestured toward the pile of files. "I know you're looking for specific links tying things together. Let me show you an interesting method for doing just that."

I raised an eyebrow, intrigued. "You read my mind."

"Observational skills, detective. Not mind-reading." She took a small step closer, and I noticed the subtle shift in her posture, a quiet confidence that was delicately attractive. She settled into a chair next to me. She was calm and relaxed. She leaned forward, her dark eyes fixed on the documents, her voice dropping to a confidential tone.

We spent the next hour dissecting the data, our voices mixing in a quiet rhythm of questions and observations. I found myself captivated not just by her intellect but by her way of thinking and her ability to organize information and connect seemingly disparate pieces.

"Nice, this is a different angle on how to link these events to the people and organizations," I said as I started to make progress with linking events and my suppositions to the artifacts on the table.

"Good, I'm glad you see the advantage to avoiding overlooping but using some loops as links between events," she said with that dynamite smile on full display.

I caught myself glancing at her several times. Each time, I risked a quick glance, hoping to catch Ji Won looking back. And each time, she did, and each time, she quickly turned away. I felt a connection growing between us.

During a few silent stretches, I began to feel the energy of unspoken possibilities taking center stage in my mind. It was disrupting my analytic psyche. I was acutely aware of her proximity, the subtle scent of her perfume more clearly discernible. It was a sophisticated blend of intensely floral and lightly tropical traces. The synergy of her eye, hair, and smile was hypnotic. The way the light caught the curve of her neck was pure visual poetry. I wanted, more than I could explain, to trace that line with my finger.

"You know," I said, breaking the silence, with my voice an octave lower than I intended, "you're very good at this."

Ji Won met my gaze, her expression unreadable for a moment, then a faint blush crept up her cheeks. "It's something I'm very passionate about."

I leaned forward slightly. "I can see that." I paused. She didn't lean away. "Passion can be an amazing driver in a person's life. It can drive us to do many things."

Her breathing deepened as we locked eyes. I could count every beat of her heart as her pulse thumped in her delicate neck. She moved closer, and I could feel the heat from her face as I looked at the beautiful curve in her lips. "Yes, passion is a driver for me too," Ji Won said, her gaze lingering on my face.

"You see things that others miss," I whispered.

She didn't pull away. Instead, she tilted her head slightly, a small, almost hesitant smile playing on her lips. "Perhaps," she admitted, her voice barely a whisper. "Or perhaps I just enjoy a good puzzle."

I reached out, almost unconsciously, and brushed a stray strand of hair from her cheek. The contact was brief and electric. Ji Won's breathing deepened as her pulse quickened, and her eyes widened slightly.

"I like your passion, it's quite compelling."

She didn't answer verbally, but the answering look in her eyes was all the confirmation I needed. I reached out with my right hand, gently touching and holding her cheek, my thumb stroking her soft skin. I waited, anticipating a flinch, but she didn't move. It was a silent invitation, and I accepted.

I lowered my head slowly, my lips hovering just above hers. I was acutely aware of her heart pounding beneath her skin, as I fought to control my own racing pulse.

The moment stretched, suspended in time, I inhaled, smelling the perfume at skin level before I finally closed the distance, my lips meeting hers in a tentative kiss. It wasn't a passionate rush, but a slow, deliberate extension of our earlier connection. If it works, it's a promise of something deeper, something more. Her arms moved around my shoulders, drawing me closer. Her breath mingled with mine.

I tasted the sweetness of her lips. I pulled back just enough to look deeply into her eyes. My heart felt like it might beat out of my chest, yet the world seemed to shrink down to just the two of us.

I leaned in again, and the kiss deepened, then I shifted down to kiss her neck as my nose touched the bottom of her earlobe.

Ji Won put her right hand on the back of my head, holding me tight as I kissed down her neck. She put her other arm over my shoulder as I twisted in my chair to face her more fully. She stepped out of her chair onto my lap, straddling me, and began kissing me more aggressively, putting her left hand on my cheek.

The intensity of the moment, fueled by the electric connection, was almost overwhelming. Ji Won's movements were deliberate and direct. The scent of her perfume, already intoxicating, was now layered with the warmth of her skin, creating a heady blend that threatened to send me into a new level of desire for her. She continued to explore, her fingers tangled in my hair, pulling gently at the strands, then her arms tightened around me, pulling me closer until we were practically fused together.

It turned out to be the best night I'd ever experienced at Wellspoint University.

# Chapter 14

I grabbed the incessantly ringing cell phone off my bedside stand.

"Good morning, Oli," I said with as much sincerity as I could muster at 5:15 a.m. while rubbing the sleep out of my eye with my left hand.

"What the hell is wrong with you, Jack!? Whhhhyy did you do that shit?" he replied, his signature, word elongation, fast talking, high-pitched voice replete with baked-in panic. Crap, did he know about Ji Won?

"What are you talking about? Everything went fine last night."

"Jack the Gazette was there, and they took pictures of yooou with Sarah and the damned mayor. Why did you dooo that?" Oli replied an octave higher than before.

"What are you worried about? I kept Sarah out of most of the pictures. Take it easy; nobody reads the newspaper anymore anyway." I said, sitting up in bed, rubbing the top of my head, just as Cooper jumped on the bed to inform me that he was in the room.

"Is this freaking thing on?" Oli screamed, and I heard Oli pounding his phone onto a table or something from the sounds of the bangs. "Listen, goofball, the Gazette is a meeeedia company with a huuuuge following on Facebook, Twitter, and you know, every social media outlet that exists. I'm looking at a picture of Youuuuu, with your arm around heeeer while the mayor looks on. Check the link I just sent you. What the hell. You know Becker's going to see this shit, and then he's going to kill me."

I put my phone on speaker and opened the link. As I scrolled through the article, my heart sank with each passing second as the weight of Oli's supposition sank in, "Oh, crap. You are Right, Oli. Well, that's just a bad angle. I don't have my arm *around her*, you know."

"Noooo, Jack, I don't know. Shit! I just got a message from Becker. He'll be at ByteStep at 8 a.m.; get your sorry ass over there, Jack!" Oli railed.

"Okay, okay, I'll check in at work then head your way, hey—" *Click. Oli hung up on me.*

In a blinding flash of ninja-like speed and agility, Cooper snuck over and grabbed the phone right out of my hand, then jumped off the bed, heading downstairs.

"Coop!" I said through an exhale, then rolled out of bed and headed downstairs, "Well, he hasn't pulled that one in a while. Crap, has everyone gone crazy around here?" I murmured to no one in particular.

Schultzy texted during my first wonderful cup of coffee while feeding Cooper. Chief Borland was awake and doing well. *That's fantastic news! Coffee cup is empty, so I'd better get moving,* I thought.

* * *

I was standing with the deputy mayor in front of me, just outside our detective's conference room.

"What is this? I'm being punished? And where is the coffee pot?" I asked, holding a piece of paper that resembled a Roman decree with an oversized signature by the deputy mayor, who was acting as Chief of Wellspoint police.

"You are being docked one day's pay for your actions yesterday. It's a disciplinary action. Think of it as a consequence of your irresponsible behavior. The coffee pot area was becoming a nuisance, too many people were carousing, making loud noises and wasting time," replied the deputy mayor dryly but with a final huff. *A literal huff.*

"Okay, how would you have preferred I handled that situation? Wait, first, people are carousing around the coffee pot? Isn't collaboration a good thing?" I replied with a tilt to my head, folding my arms across my chest.

"First of all, you can handle the situation by being thorough enough the first time through so there's not an abrupt change at the last minute that puts our elected leaders in a difficult public position. You mismanaged the situation; you need to think about using proper processes, proper planning, and effective follow-through." He said through an exhale while waving his left hand in a circular motion. "Second, you'll soon see, removing that disgusting tar pit caffeination apparatus will be a boon for productivity."

I dropped my arms and handed him the paper. I cocked my head at him and smiled, saying in a whisper, "Are you making this up, just. To. You know, bother me?"

Before he could respond, Sergeant Bartlett walked by, drawing both of our attention. Sergeant Bartlett stopped, turned around, and walked back toward the deputy mayor and me. He then stepped halfway between us, "Detective, can you join me in the squad room? I have a few items to get sorted out and could use your help."

I looked at Sergeant Bartlett and then back to the deputy mayor. "Sure, Sarge, let's go; this isn't going anywhere that's for sure," I said with a smirk, pointing at the deputy mayor and myself.

"Yes, let's get out there and do some good, you two. Make our city safe from the criminal vermin leaking in from out of town!" the deputy mayor said with a thumbs-up before abruptly striding away.

We entered the squad room, a thirty-foot-by-thirty-foot, brightly lit room where uniformed officers met, prepared, and collaborated. The room was filled with numerous footlockers, tables, and cabinets, all strewn with a wide variety of police equipment and uniform parts. It smelled like Pine-Sol and shoe polish, giving off a locker room vibe. I followed Sergeant Bartlett into a corner where a table held a small Keurig Coffee maker.

"Here we go; he never comes in here; it stinks to him," Sergeant Bartlett said as he smiled, then he popped in a coffee cartridge and pressed the brew button. Then he handed me a fresh cup of Colombian express black coffee, popping in a fresh cartridge to make a cup for himself.

I smiled broadly, nodding, "Thanks, this is exactly what the doctor ordered. The deputy mayor seems to be a bit of a clock maker, where everything's gotta be just so."

Sergeant Bartlett nodded. "I suspect Chief Borland will be back in a day or two. He may have a different viewpoint on docking your pay. By the way, Agent Jenkins left a message for you. Hold on a sec," he set his coffee down and began flipping through papers on his ever-present clipboard. "Here it is, 'Stapletoes said it was a tall, blond female, mid-twenties, long, straight hair, square shoulders, attractive. No name, though.' I presume you know what he's talking about?"

"I do; that's interesting news. Thank you. If he calls back, can you tell 'em Christina is a computer?" I replied. "He'll know what I mean."

Sergeant Bartlett wrote down the message and gave me a thumbs up, "Roger, will do, detective."

"Any word on Miokin, Spake, or any of his band of merry men? I've been checking with all my contacts, and it's like they disappeared. I really want to get my hands on Miokin." I asked with a furrowed brow and after a sip of coffee.

"I can imagine. I asked for an update from the state and bureau first thing this morning. State's got nothing new, and the bureau hasn't responded yet. I think it's a little early in the morning for those boys and girls."

I snickered, "Very likely, Sergeant B., very likely indeed. Thanks for this, and I appreciate your help with messaging Jenkins." I said, pointing at the paper cup full of Colombian coffee.

He grinned back with those oversized front teeth, set above his strong chin that anchored his weathered face. Then he walked away with the clipboard under his arm and a coffee cup in his other hand. He started a discussion with two officers waiting to use the Keurig, asking how their morning had started. *Sergeant Bartlett is a great mentor for the junior officers.*

My phone chimed with a new message from Oli: "911GET OVER HERE!"

I decided to skip round two with Deputy Hardass and strode out the door of the police station. On my way out, I heard a faint "Hey, where'd you get that coffee, detective?" I turned to see two operations staffers. I recognized one as a dispatcher, a particularly tough job without coffee. "Quietly talk with the Desk Sergeant," I yelled in reply, then turned and walked out the door.

* * *

I walked up the steps to ByteStep computers, which still had the closed sign lit and in place up front. I noticed Sarah's car was not there yet, so I jogged up the stairs, and when I got into the lobby, I found a very nervous Oliver Knight talking with a six-foot wall of muscle, Michael Becker, a fortyish-year-old, former biker and MMA fighter, who had turned to union work, leading several organizations in the area, including construction workers regional 447, machinists 126, and numerous individuals involved in local excavation work, such as those at the local gravel pit. A lot of muscle and fighting know-how stood inches from the diminutive Oliver Knight. I had to do something to distract him.

"Someone called the police?" I said with a friendly smile and closed the door behind me.

Becker turned, seeing that I had entered the room, bolted in my direction. He stopped in front of me, then we stood face to face. I could see the veins in his temple pulsing and veins creeping up his neck and cheeks starting to show as he cracked his knuckles. "What the hell are you doing with my little girl, Stewart? I'm going to give you thirty seconds—"

I cut him off, "Take it easy, Becker, everyone in this room is helping your daughter," I said, not using her name. Oli quietly walked over to the door and locked it.

"Oh yeah, how?! She texted me a couple of times this week, and this morning. Said she's really into her work and a new guy," he grunted.

I looked over at Oli, as I had *no* idea how much Oli had told him about what was going on.

"She's doing a great job with the forensics analysis work, you should be proooud of her," Oli said as he warily walked over toward us, but stopped a careful couple of meters away. "She's even helping Jack with a special assignment."

"Let's go, Stewart. What's she helping you with? Because I saw a picture texted to me this morning that looked like you were out on a fucking date with my daughter."

"No, that's not it at all. She and I... well, we went to the university to collect some data, see, and well, there were some pictures taken, but those were innocent pictures. Honestly, Becker, I wouldn't do anything to hurt your daughter. Oli here's given her a great job where she can get some experience in a field she's interested in—"

Becker cut me off and put his massive right hand on my left shoulder. "Collecting some data, huh? Let me tell you something," he squeezed my shoulder, causing me to wince, "if I find out you are messing with my little girl, you won't make it out of the next room we're in together."

I shrugged his hand off my shoulder with a powerful move and inched forward, looking down at him. Then, in the plainest, flattest tone I could muster, I said, "I'm not dating your daughter; I'm not hurting her, and she's helping me with a case. A murder case. It's important. And she's doing a really good job. You have my word."

"Oooookay, you two," Oli broke in from a distance, "Let's not get tooooo worked up here. Lots of expensive things." Oli's voice quivered, "Becker, Sarah is fine; she's doing greeeeat, and she's getting exposure over at the university."

Becker turned to look at Oli, causing him to step back up a half step, "What kind of exposure?"

I replied, "People like her, the kind of people she wants to be around, not like us. They are educated in computer science. It's good. She's learning and having fun," I said, backing up a step out of his personal space. I could see the veins in his neck recede as his level of agitation seemed to abate slightly.

Becker looked down and rubbed his chin with his right hand, then his eyes darted between Oli and me, and the room went silent for a full thirty seconds. "If you find out who is dating her, I'd like to know."

I nodded once. We stood there in a moment of silence with nobody moving.

Finally, he looked at Oli and said, "She still doesn't know that I asked you for this favor, right?"

Oli stepped forward bravely and replied, "That, that's right, she doesn't know. But it's greeeeat to hear she's been teeexting you."

A bunch of large and small dogs started barking incessantly just outside the front of the ByteStep building. There must have been seven or eight of them, just barking away as someone honked a horn.

We stood there quietly for a moment. Then Oli stuttered out a quivering sentence, "Wow, I wonder who, who let the dogs out."

Typical Oli, always trying to figure out a way to jibber jabber. I face-palmed, furrowing my brow at his goofy statement, then I glanced over toward Becker. "We're looking out for her, and we'll be on the lookout for her boyfriend," I said with a half-smile.

Becker's phone chimed with two messages, causing him to glance at his phone to read them. Finally, he glanced one more time between Oli and me, "Okay, well, I've got to get to work. Talk with you two another time."

As he turned to walk out the door, Oli quickly scooted out of the way and deftly unlocked the door so Becker wouldn't have to. "Okay, Becker, we'll see you next time." Oli stammered.

As the door shut behind Becker, Oli exhaled, doubling over, then stood back up. "Okay, see, I had that all under control. What did I tell you, Jackie my boy, everything is juuuuust fine."

"Oh for…. You've been freaking out for like the past three hours!" I exclaimed.

His eyes looked to the ceiling for a few seconds, then back down to me. "Ahhh, okay, maybe just a pinch," he said, using his right hand's index finger and thumb to form a pinching motion over and over again.

I shook my head from side to side, "Okay, Oli, I have to go. I'm meeting Dr. Turner over at the university. Please ask Sarah to let me know when she finds something relevant, good, or bad. No waiting until the last minute."

"Hey, don't forget the Cincinnati game tonight. I'll see you at Tower's," Oli said as I started for the door.

I stopped and turned back toward Oli. I extended my arms and turned the palms of my hands up, "Are we telling Daddy about the boyfriend?"

Oli's eyes went to the ground as if the answer was written on the floor, and then turned back to me with his eyes wide open and said, "Hell no. I'm not going there; besides, you are taking care of that problem."

"I am?" I replied. "I thought you were going to handle it?"

"Yes, yes, that's what I meant, us, we, you and me, weeee are going to handle it. We've got this under control," Oli said, pointing his left hand at himself, then toward me, then back to himself. The forced cheerfulness felt brittle; it didn't inspire confidence. When Becker learned who was actually dating his daughter and what he'd done to her, we'd all be in trouble. A cold certainty settled over me. This wasn't just about keeping a secret about Sarah's boyfriend or keeping her safe. This was about navigating a minefield that included perceptions of Sarah's situation. It all started to feel like a lead jacket suffocating me under the combined weight of the murder investigation, Sarah's involvement, and the deputy mayor's conduct.

Walking to my car, I caught a glimpse of a dark, late-model SUV parked across the street. It was angled toward the building, as if waiting for someone. The tinted windows made it impossible to see inside, but a gut feeling told me it wasn't there by chance. It was a feeling I couldn't shake. Someone was watching. And I had a feeling they weren't on my side.

# Chapter 15

"He's dead, detective," said a somber-faced Sergeant Capwell, standing in the center of the street at the main intersection of the university access road and highway 214. "It happened about fifteen minutes ago. I just got here myself, about five minutes after the ambulance. Dr. Turner was hit hard." The sun was beating down on us, reflecting off the asphalt like a bad omen. Sergeant Capwell's face was etched with concern as sweat beaded across both our foreheads.

"What do we know?" I replied, scanning the scene, wiping the sweat from my forehead. There was a bicycle sitting about fifteen feet in front of the car that struck it, pounding it into a twisted pretzel of metal and tire rubber, with the body covered by a sheet about ten feet further forward than the bicycle. Onlookers were standing at the edges of all four streets. The place was swamped with people trying to get a look at what had happened, as the smell of burned engine coolant cut through the clean scent of fresh-cut grass along the university side of the street. This was a university access road, not really a high-speed area.

"Not much, I'm yellow taping the scene and holding the driver until you tell me what to do with him. Those two students were crossing the street when they saw a grey Dodge sports car run a red light and hit the professor at high speed. The driver claims he didn't see the cyclist. That's about all I've gotten so far. The driver is standing over there by the ambulance." He replied, pointing toward the median.

"Thanks, Cap, let me interview them and circle back in a few minutes," I said. "When others show up, ask one of them to start interviews on that side of the street. I'll start over here." Two more police cars arrived, and, after conferring with Sergeant Capwell, the officers assumed their assigned roles.

My gut knotted as I bent over and examined the body of Dr. Turner, lying in a painfully twisted position with one leg and one arm wrenched unnaturally around his body, a position no yoga instructor would ever recommend.

The scene launched painful memories of my time in the war. People you know one day are just fucking gone the next. No warning, no messages, just gone. A vivid reminder that every soldier knows well. We are just temporary bits of squishy entropy in this world. *All the better reason to try to do some good,* I always thought.

Blood from Turner's head was everywhere, clinging to his body and running downhill toward the street where several students stood silently, looking at the river of blood. His eyes were sunken into his head, frozen in a permanent state of shock and pain.

I stood up and slowly walked back toward the sidewalk, thinking about the situation. Before I finished interviewing the tenth eyewitness, out of the corner of my eye, I recognized a person in the modulating sea of faces, all looking at the coroner team that was handling the body. *Russell Spake, Miokin's right-hand man, what was he doing here?*

I carefully put my notebook and pen away and stepped backwards nonchalantly out of the thick crowd of people I was in. Then, without warning, I turned and bolted across the street toward Spake, dodging pedestrians and leaping over obstacles.

He saw me and took off running down the street toward the university, putting his cell phone to his head. I heard guffaws and screams as Spake pushed people out of his way, sometimes pushing them to the ground.

I was gaining on him as he sprinted in the open down a side street and toward a multi-level parking garage.

"Spake! Stop! Police!" I yelled, passing numerous students who all stepped back onto the grass from the walkway to avoid me as I blasted by.

When I reached the parking garage, I went up the stairs on one end and down the stairs at the other, asking people if they had seen a man running by wearing a blue shirt and grey Dockers. No one had any sight of him. The concrete walls seemed to close in on me, with the sounds of students chatting and cars passing through the building. I went back downstairs and did a couple of circles around the garage but couldn't find any signs of Spake.

Walking back to the scene, I began to think about why Spake would have been at the university.

"You okay, detective?" asked Sergeant Capwell, holding out a bottle of water, which I took and downed in two huge gulps.

"Yeah, I'm okay. Thanks for the water. I didn't get him. Lost him in the damn parking garage. It was Russell Spake, Miokin's right-hand man." I replied as I wiped sweat from my forehead. I looked around at the scene. The body was gone, and the road was partially cleared, with one of the uniformed officers directing traffic around the police cars.

"I had the car towed and the driver is in my back seat," he replied, nodding toward his police cruiser parked along the edge of the street.

I glanced at his police cruiser and then back to Sergeant Capwell, "Thanks, Cap, I'm going to talk with him for a sec, be right back."

I walked over and opened the cruiser's back door, and he stepped out of the car. Male, about five feet eight inches, skinny, oversized brown eyes, dark shoulder-length hair, large ears for his head and a goatee covering his chin.

"Officer, I sure am sorry about hitting that man. I did *not* see him until it was too late," he said with a slight European accent that I couldn't quite pin down, *maybe German.*

I nodded, looking from him toward the scene and then back to him, "What is your name?"

"Damian, Damian Willis," He replied

"Was that Dodge your car, Damian?"

"No," he replied, putting his thumbs into his front jeans pockets, his eyes darting back and forth as they skipped nervously up and down the street, avoiding eye contact.

"Where'd you get the car?" I asked.

"I borrowed it from a friend last night. Needed to run some errands," he replied, stepping backward to light a cigarette from which he then took a long drag.

I nodded, looking away, then back toward him, "You live around here, Damian? You got family here?"

"No, sir, I'm staying over on Cutter Road, Garden Apartments. No family, sir."

"What brings you over to the university this morning? You late for class?" I asked, pointing over my shoulder toward the university.

"Nothing.  I just got turned around and mixed up," he replied, pointing to the other direction. He then turned, looking back in the opposite direction. I noticed a small black and red scorpion tattoo on his neck near the collar of his shirt. He took another drag on the cigarette as he shrugged his shoulders.

"Can I see your driver's license, Damian?"

He nodded, placing the cigarette into his mouth, and then fished his very empty wallet from his back pocket. Plucked out his driver's license and handed it to me.

"Where do you work, Damian?" I said, returning his New York license.

"Well, I'm sort of between gigs at the moment, just finished a stint in New York at the container terminal. Hard work but good money,"

"Damian, a man died here today, so I've got some tough questions for you. I'm going to look you right in the eyes. Did you recognize anyone at the scene here? Any of the girls? Students? Guys?" I asked, shifting my weight onto one leg and staring straight into his eyes.

"Uhhh, no, I uhh… didn't really recognize anyone here," he replied, rubbing his chin and flicking his cigarette away behind the police cruiser.

"How about the man riding the bicycle? Did you recognize him?" I was still locked onto his eyes with mine.

Damian fidgeted his feet as his eyes constricted just a millisecond before looking away toward where the cyclist lay before the coroner team took his body away. "No, sir, I did not know him."

I kept staring as Damian shifted around on his feet but continued to meet my gaze. Ten, then fifteen seconds ticked by as I stared into his eyes.

"That's not what I asked Damian. I asked if you recognized him. There's a difference."

"Yes, sir. Sorry about that. No, I did not recognize him."

I nodded and looked back toward Sergeant Capwell, then back toward Damian.

"Sir, can I go now? I need to get going, it's been hours."

"Damian, please have a seat back in the car. I'll be right back." I said, opening the door and motioning for him to sit. I walked back over to Sergeant Capwell, considering everything that had occurred.

I inhaled then exhaled fully, "Cap, can you do me a favor. Take him in and book him for homicide? I want to continue speaking with a few of the witnesses here. Then I'll be in to do the paperwork."

Sergeant Capwell nodded and asked, "Homicide or manslaughter?"

"Homicide," I replied. "And Cap, be careful. Make sure someone goes with you or at least follows you back to the station. Something's not right about this guy. And we've got some bold, European criminals going after cops the last couple of days."

Sergeant Capwell stood up a little straighter, pushed his chin out, glanced across the street toward Damian, and then replied, "Yes, sir, consider it done."

* * *

Two hours later, I was sitting in my office, completing research on Damian Willis after submitting my incident report on Dr. Turner. I was reviewing details from the second interview with Willis. His cell phone was very sparse, with only a digital currency wallet, two social media apps and a gambling app outstanding from the standard app suite.

Angie walked into the tiny, poorly lit space and sat down on the chair in front of my desk. She looked at the pottery pieces on my desk and picked one up. "This is an interesting piece, I've always wondered about its origin, Jack," she said with a weak smile and a furrowed brow.

"That is what we call a coil pot in the pottery world," I said with a weary crinkle forming in the corners of my eyes. "You roll out long ropes of clay and stack them, then blend them together in a sort of smearing motion."

"Huh, I always thought it was from a niece or nephew, so you made this... piece of art?" she said as her voice trailed an octave higher.

I chuckled. "I did. I made it during a wine and art date with Ginger a long time ago. She liked doing those events. They weren't bad," I said, looking over Angie's shoulder in recollection of that date night.

Angie set the pot back onto the desk, nodding affirmatively, leaned back, folding one leg over the other and rubbing her hands together gently. "Just read your report. Folks at the University are pretty freaked out about Dr. Turner's death. You are holding this guy Willis on homicide?"

I leaned forward onto my elbows and gave her a half smile and nodded. She cocked her head and continued, "Look, Jack, I know you and I haven't always seen eye to eye, but the prosecutor's going to want more than what we have. Are you thinking clearly on this one? I don't think we need to make extra work for people around here."

I pushed my keyboard away and leaned back in my seat, considering her words. Then I frowned, shaking my head from side to side, "Twenty witnesses say he ran a red light and hit Turner at high speed. Something big is happening here, and we've got to get ahead of it. These are very dangerous and bold criminals. They're getting help, and I think, high-level protection."

Angie looked at me, shifted in her seat and then nodded affirmatively.

"I also just read some interesting research on Dr. Turner. He was quite the businessman, not sure why he shifted his career into education, but his death is certainly a sad turn of events. Angie, I'm pretty sure this was *not* a random accident. Russell Spake was at the scene today. I missed him, lost him during a foot pursuit. This guy, Damian, I think he knows more than he's telling us. He was definitely going too fast, and he claims he was lost. Most folks drive slower than the speed limit when they are lost. He has just arrived in town and has very few contacts on his brand-new cell phone. I think he recognized Dr. Turner. I think it was a hit, not an accident."

Angie's feet fidgeted as she shifted her legs and nodded. "Motive?"

"Not sure but I've got a brewing theory."

"How can I help? What's the theory?"

"The Union specializes in currency management, theft and such. We have a dead computer science expert and his dead student, who worked on the computer system that runs the casino's financial and security systems. It's starting to come together for me, but I need a few questions answered, though. What I need is an honest conversation with the casino owner," I said. "I need to get him to talk and provide information about who's running their fancy new computer system called Christina."

Angie smiled, then put both feet on the floor, bounced her hand off the desk, "Okay, I think I can get that audience, without a subpoena, I hope. I need to go back to the casino anyway. I'm at a dead end with Miokin, and we've checked the cameras all around the university, looking for anyone bringing Spake in or out. There are no signs. Nothing. Topping it off, the Bureau isn't exactly helping. Your ex, Ginger, isn't being helpful either. She's stopped responding to questions. At first, I thought she was hiding something. But now I think it's just overwhelming for her. Still, given her background, she should be able to respond more effectively. I don't know what's going on with her. Maybe you can help me with that. You two have been apart for what, a month?" Angie asked with a furrowed brow.

I nodded. "We split six weeks ago. Yep, planning to get a hold of her. Things seem to keep popping up."

"Well, you've had a long, rough afternoon. Why don't you get out of here? We'll link up here in the morning and head over to the casino. Oh, not sure if you heard yet, Chief is doing pretty well, may show up for a half day tomorrow," she replied with a smile.

I smiled back with a genuine, full-faced grin of appreciation.

She looked down at me and cocked her head sideways just a tick and said, "Go get some rest, Jack," Angie said, then turned and walked out of my office.

* * *

"You look terrible, buddy. Here's a cold beer. That ought to lighten you up a notch," said Oli, smiling broadly as I sat down at our customary table in Towers pub. The Cincinnati Reds were on every screen, playing the Milwaukee Brewers, and there was a lot of chatter and excitement as the game was midway through and a high-scoring affair, 6–8 in favor of the Brewers. Tower raised his voice an octave, "Oh, C'mon

Roberto, it's not brain surgery; it's a baseball, just hit the damn thing. Gee whiz, he's 0-for-4 tonight," he grimaced as Roberto De La Cruz, the Reds' second baseman, took strike three and started walking to the dugout.

"Yeah, Jack, what's going on?" Tower said between chews as he worked on a chicken sandwich.

I laid out the bulk of my day to Oli and Tower, highlighting the loss of Dr. Turner, a kind professor with significant influence and a substantial amount of money, who worked at a one-horse university building tech to license with the private sector and even the government. There was a lot that didn't add up. But for now, I tried to give them some honest background and then make it all about the Reds' game, rather than being a downer to my buddies.

"Alright, Alright, enough with the work doom and gloom, Jackie." Oli chuckled, wiping barbecue sauce from his cheek. "You are the best detective in the state, Jack. If anybody can sort this out, it's you. Now, let's focus on something we all can control, and that's whether the Reds can claw their way back from this hole they've dug for themselves."

I nodded affirmatively, fake-smiled at his attempt to pick me up. I'd been a detective too long not to know things could still get worse. A dead student, a dead professor, faked data, a string of kidnappings and simultaneous attacks on cops and the Feds. The implications of it all pressed down on me. I'd been a detective too long, seen too much ugliness, to believe things couldn't get worse. The casual cheer of the pub felt like a suffocating mask, hiding the dark reality of organized crime moving into my city. My gut twisted: a silent scream warning me that the game wasn't just on the screens, it was on for me, and the stakes were far higher than any baseball score.

# Chapter 16

Emily ushered Angie and me into the casino owner's office, which was spacious, plush, and smelled vaguely floral, a stark contrast to Lucas Flynn's office, which was a technically focused space filled with steel furniture, electronics, and massive smart glass windows looking out over the casino floor. Malachi Hunter gave us a nod, then stood from the head of a beautiful, rectangular, marble-topped table that seated nine, positioned in the center of his wonderfully manicured office, which was replete with green plants and brightly colored flowers.

"Mr. Hunter, we appreciate you taking the time to see us today," I said as we were ushered in. I made a beeline for him and shook his hand, smiling at the others in the room. "I think you all know Detective Angie Heist."

"Yes, and I think you both know my casino manager, Lucas Flynn, and our chief of casino security, Carson Porter. This is our general counsel, Evan Howe," Hunter added.

I shook everyone's hand, ending with Evan Howe, a smartly dressed fellow about five feet ten inches, with bright brown eyes, jet-black hair, neatly trimmed over his ears, and a pointy chin. Howe's appearance was distinguished by the large, aquiline nose that seemed a bit too large for his face. He wore a business suit with fine details, including a kerchief in his breast pocket and cufflinks with a complex, unidentifiable design.

Everything about him said "meticulous."

"Mr. Hunter, we would like to get a look at Christina to set some context for our discussion."

Hunter's smile didn't quite reach his eyes. "Christina is...," he paused, his gaze sweeping the room. Carson Porter shifted slightly, and Evan Howe's jaw clenched. "A critical asset. Let's get straight to what you need." Malachi Hunter's smile vanished, his expression hardening as he raised a finger, silencing the room. The foursome shifted toward a corner of the room and circled around Evan Howe. They subtly pivoted their voices to a murmur that I couldn't quite make out. Malachi Hunter finally gave the group a thumbs-up. Carson then put his cell phone to his ear, his face grim, eyes darting between Angie, me and Malachi. My unexpected request hit the foursome like I'd asked for naked pictures of their wives, unexpected, and perhaps out of bounds.

"Yes, detective, we'll show you the data center and try to give you some details along the way, but it may not provide as much insight as you are hoping for. Lucas is calling our CTO to arrange a *quick* tour." Malachi looked toward the red-headed chief of casino security and said, "Are we good, Carson?"

"Yes, we are. Austin will meet us there," the pudgy redhead said with a forced smile.

"Thanks; okay, detectives, if you'll follow me, we'll give you the nickel tour," Malachi said, smiling broadly.

We walked a circuitous route, down three flights of stairs as Malachi narrated, "You may not be aware, but the Fantasy Casino is built on the site of an old elementary school. We were able to leverage much of the building's basement architecture, and power and water infrastructure," he continued talking as we entered a checkpoint where two very large, uniformed security guards with shotguns, and another gentleman greeted us. "Austin, this is detectives Stewart and Heist," he said, pointing between Angie and me. "Detectives, this is our CTO, Austin

Vaughn. He's been with the company since the beginning."

Austin scanned Angie and me with his eyes and then stepped forward, extending his hand for a shake.

*So I shook it.*

He was about five feet ten inches tall, with dark, shoulder-length hair, a skinny, almost gaunt body, and a face with piercing brown eyes, a sharp jawline, and high cheekbones that gave him an eerie, stressed, and workaholic vibe.

"That's right, employee number three," Austin said as he shook Angie's hand.

"Great to meet you, albeit under bad circumstances," I replied.

The larger of the two security guards walked over to me and Angie and ran a wand up and down our bodies, stopping at our firearms. The big guy didn't say anything as he just held out a tray that said "Weapons Locker" on it.

I glanced at Angie and then pulled my Glock out and placed it on the tray. His wand didn't reach my backup Smith & Wesson .38, so that was a bonus. I didn't anticipate much trouble heading into a data center anyway. Angie put her Sig Sauer onto the tray and then smiled at the guard, which elicited a grunt from the big fellow.

"Come, let's give you an overview of what makes the Fantasy Casino special," he said with a bright smile, then turned and walked through the checkpoint door.

I detected a slight European accent but decided to background that for the moment.

We continued walking down the long, grey corridor, which was devoid of sound except for our shoes scraping along the rough concrete. It was stale-smelling and devoid of features, except for massive, ceiling-mounted cable looms filled with all manner of wires and fiber optics on one side, and pipes, presumably carrying water, on the other side of the ceiling.

We'd walked about 200 meters down the leftward curving corridor when we came up to another door, which Austin opened using his badge and by punching in a pin code on the door's security panel. "This is it; we call it the cafeteria, c'mon in."

We entered a huge, brightly lit rectangular room. Eight people worked at computer desks on one side, while another six people sat on the other side, with ten or so desks remaining unoccupied. At the far end, I could see a massive, glass-enclosed room filled with server racks. I counted seven rows, each with at least five racks. The air was dry, and the smell of ozone hung heavy, making my eyes itch.

I scanned the room, the unnatural lighting bouncing off the white, painted concrete floor. "Why a cafeteria?" I asked, my voice echoing slightly in the cavernous room. We all entered the front end of the room and formed a loose semi-circle around Austin.

"Well, this used to be a school cafeteria that also doubled as a tornado shelter because it's in a deep basement. On the left side is primarily our software integrators: folks that work with the university to install, update and maintain Christina."

I nodded. "How about those folks on the other side of the room?"

Austin looked toward Evan and Malachi, then back to me, "That's the CISO's security operations team. They provide security overwatch for Christina and all the network infrastructure on premises."

"I see, so your data center back there houses everything; you don't lease infrastructure in the hyperscaler clouds off-prem?"

"No, detective, that got us into trouble before. Too easy to compro-mise."

Evan stepped forward and chimed in, "Detective, we'll give you details on that later if you don't mind."

"Sure, no problem, Evan," I replied with a smile and a nod.

We stepped toward the large, kiosk-like desk in the center of the space, which featured a large central monitor and two smaller side monitors. It had numerous cables and systems plugged into it from adjacent boxes. Austin raised it to a standing position, then motioned for us to crowd around him. "Here, I'm bringing up a console session with Christina." He placed the headset on and clicked away at the keyboard until an avatar appeared on the primary monitor. The face was very skinny, made from a wire mesh, and it was apparently talking to Austin through the headset. Slowly, as the seconds passed, the wire mesh began to be covered with a cross-hatched pattern of light, medium, and dark green colors until the face looked slightly more human than before. I couldn't quite make out what he was typing, but finally Austin backed away and handed me the headphones.

"Here you go, detective. I'll let you say hi, and then you can pass the headset to Detective Heist. This is a console connection, so it's you and Christina, albeit with a log of events being recorded," he said, pointing his thumb in the direction of the glass-enclosed data center.

I put the headset on and said hello, looking at the green-faced female avatar. It looked a lot like a green-skinned Ava Gardner, except with slightly larger eyes and a touch less hair.

"Hello, Detective Jack Stewart of the Wellspoint Police Department. I'm Christina, a machine intelligence entity. How can I assist you?"

I furrowed my brow, hardly able to believe how realistic that sounded. The tone, tenor, and pace of the deeply female voice were incredibly lifelike. "Uhh, Hi Christina. I'm on a case and just trying to learn about the casino and you a little," I said, not really knowing what to say.

"I can tell you everything that's occurring: there are 172 guests in the main floor casino, 3,770 online participants in private auctions, live fantasy events, and entertainment activities. The Casino is up 1.33 million dollars for the day, and there are no operational anomalies detected. Only 4,718 network attacks have occurred today, all blocked."

I smiled. "Wow, that's a lot of attacks to track. How do you do it? You can't even see, can you?" I asked, smiling over at Angie, then glancing back at the avatar.

"I see very well. I can see you, Detective Stewart; look into the camera on top of the monitor. Yes." Christina replied with a deepening husky female voice.

My smile drained away. "Did you know Dr. Turner's face?" I replied.

"Yes, of course, he's one of my two core admins."

"Two? Who's the other?"

"Brent Savvoy"

My eyes narrowed. "Isn't Austin a core admin?"

"No, he is an Administrator, but not of the core. Do you have any other questions?"

I exhaled slowly but thoroughly, "What is your mission?" I replied, looking right into the camera with a half-smile.

"My mission is to maintain optimal casino operations, ensuring financial integrity and safeguarding against all threats, both internal and external, by actively monitoring and neutralizing any potential disruptions."

"Interesting, what is the last disruption you neutralized?"

"I identified a customer attempting to exploit a fantasy experience server, blocked the requests and removed the customer from active status."

"Well, I guess you solved that problem?" I nodded, smiling more fully, glancing toward the assembled group to my left.

"Not really. That customer will likely create numerous new accounts and try again. I am an expert at identity exploitation and prioritize these types of malicious attempts. Do you have any other questions, detective?"

I stood up a little straighter and looked into the camera. "No, not now," I said, taking the headset off so Angie could talk with Christina.

I turned to Austin, looking around at the room, then shuffling away from the group. That last comment put me back into detective mode.

"Christina indicated she handled thousands of network attacks today. How can that be if all your infrastructure is in here with the handheld Sparrows?"

"We have many online customers accessing from remote locations via web browsers. They come from all over the world; the servers are here, but they are proxied through cache servers hosted for us by WPF Net downtown."

I nodded, recognizing the local ISP provider name, Wellspoint Fox Net. They send me a bill for internet service each month. Angie laughed at the screen, nodding as the group collapsed around her. I could barely make out a chart on the screen.

"So this area is obviously very secure. Are there any emergency exits?" I asked

Austin pointed toward the emergency exit door near the data center, "Yes, that door goes straight up three flights or so of stairs to the parking lot."

"What are those nozzles in the ceiling for? Shouldn't they only be inside the enclosure where the server racks are?" I replied, thinking about Brent Savvoy's untimely death.

"We have a robust fire suppression system in place," Austin said, his voice tight, "A significant loss to any of these systems would be... untenable," as he pointed at several larger systems in the room.

Angie removed the headset and started laughing, talking with Malachi and Evan, who were overseeing her session with Christina.

"Austin, did you know Professor Turner? I mean, it's odd that both he's dead, and one of the students who was central to building Christina."

Austin looked over my shoulder at the others and then back to me. His eyes moistened as he replied, "Ira was my best friend. I'm privately devastated. Trying to hold it together," he said quietly, then turned to look at the ground.

I pressed my lips together, nodding.

"Okay, let's head back to the conference room," said Malachi as he walked over and patted Austin on the back.

I used the long walk back to the conference room to learn more about Austin. He was a gifted mathematician in college and had originally moved from New York City to Wellspoint to build the fantasy casino at the behest of Malachi.

"Please, everyone, have a seat," Hunter motioned, indicating the table. "Before we get started, would anyone like something to drink?" A woman with a drink cart moved behind the table, serving Mr. Hunter and Evan. I asked for a Diet Coke, and Angie took a small bottle of water, and we sat down.

"Detective Stewart, we might not be able to help you with everything you want to know, but given Dr. Turner's death and the activity at the university, we want to help as much as possible. Please ask your questions."

I looked over at Angie and then said, "Okay, how long has Christina been up and running at the Fantasy Casino here in Wellspoint?"

Malachi Hunter looked at Evan, who nodded. "Currently," Mr. Hunter said, "Christina has been fully functional for about ninety days. There was a phased transition from the previous system, which we are still using parts of."

"May I ask why you decided to upgrade or change computer systems or architectures?" I asked.

Hunter replied, "Yes, there was an incident. Our private security team handled the matter in collaboration with a computer security firm based in New York. Here's our *internal* report. We did not file a report with the police as we handled the situation with our private security." Evan pushed two copies of a report across the table to Angie and me, "So we can talk about this if you like. It's quite sensitive. The fact is, our previous service provider was caught facilitating internal computer system access to criminals who eventually ransomware'd our system, holding it hostage from us."

I nodded as I flipped through the report, noticing some interesting details and a crap ton of thick black redactions. I glanced at Angie and looked back at Mr. Hunter. "So, bad guys got a hold of your previous system, encrypted aspects of it, and forced you to pay to remove the encryption?"

Evan Howe jumped in, "Look, detective, we can't get into too many details. A large number of transactions occur daily across our architecture. This is one of four Fantasy Casino sites directly connected, facilitating millions of currency conversions and custom currency transactions per day between the four sites. The plumbing is highly confidential."

I raised my left eyebrow at the sudden outburst by the casino's lawyer, "Okay, is it the same service provider running Christina?"

Malachi Hunter replied quickly, "No. We sued the original service provider for allowing an insider to provide system access to criminals. They fought it, though, claiming that an employee had gone rogue. At that point, we didn't think we could trust any service provider. Well-connected criminal organizations have a lot of opportunities to gain leverage inside these large companies."

"Okay, I think I understand. An insider enabled access to your computer system, which bad guys ransomed because your service provider let them in the front door, digitally speaking. And Austin runs Christina now, correct?"

Malachi Hunter looked at Evan, who responded, "Yes, we've developed our own staff by hiring experts, and even hiring from the local university, essentially building our own full-time service provider and security staff to run Christina, providing security and oversight."

I nodded with a firm half smile, "Okay, but did police ever arrest or identify who ransomware'd the casino?"

Malachi's eyes narrowed. He quickly glanced around the room, straightened up, and said, "We don't know. But we're pretty sure it was an organized crime group."

I nodded. "Do you know which group or organization it was?"

Malachi replied, "Not specifically, but we were informed that there was an associate with a group called the Union. That's what we were told by our private security and the cybersecurity response firm that helped us restore our original system."

"So, currently, are there no bad guys in your new system?" I asked, looking at Evan with a furrowed brow.

Evan shook his head, and Malachi answered, "Detective, we're not going to answer that. We are extending ourselves here to help you with a murder case."

"Two murder cases," I replied, looking at Evan, then glancing at Malachi. I looked over at Angie, then back at Evan. "What was the precise nature of the original breach, if I might ask?"

Evan spoke up. "As we told you, it was a ransomware breach. The actor was expelled, and we changed our architecture to be more resilient."

"But you can't confirm for me that there are no actors currently in your system?"

Evan shifted in his seat and looked at Jack, about to speak, when Malachi cut in. "Look, detective, the criminals not only ransomware'd our system's core and our transaction database, but it's possible they also used parts of our architecture designed for gaming to conduct their own business for a period of time without our knowledge. That's all we are going to say on the subject. It's complicated."

I looked between Malachi and Evan, nodding slowly. "Okay, for the record, I recently had a run-in with some bad guys associated with the Union not too long ago. Dmitri Myoken, Russell Spake, either of those names ring a bell?"

Evan didn't move, and Malachi didn't say anything, simply nodding slowly from side to side.

"Okay, well, I'm looking for them, so if you see or hear from them, can you please let me know? I want to *talk* with them," I said with a wolfish grin.

Evan and Malachi glanced at one another. Their silence felt brittle. *Need to shift the focal point and break the tension in the room.*

"How well did you know Professor Ira Turner?"

"I knew him pretty well. We worked together to install and configure Christina," said Malachi, glancing across the room toward Austin.

"Interesting," I said. "Would you say that Professor Turner was an expert on that system?"

Malachi looked at Austin, and then Evan answered, "Yes, Dr. Turner helped design and build the system for us. Through a contract with the university, he was one of the lead architects for the entire platform."

"Part of your private service provider staff, then. Okay, did you have Professor Turner's students working on Christina?"

"Yes," said Evan. "I don't specifically remember any of them. There were numerous students in and out. Some of this was considered research for them. To my knowledge, a few ended up becoming employees, those with the aptitude and desire to be on the Casino's team."

"So, did Dr. Turner accompany them each time?"

"That's right, and they were escorted by our staff," Evan said. "Only Dr. Turner and one other student had credentials to Christina; the students were never in danger."

I nodded, writing down details in my notebook. "Okay, let me see if I've got this right. Your computer system got hacked, bad guys got in, ransomware'd part of it, and while they were ransom-wearing it, they were also using it for their own needs. When you found out, you fired the service provider and brought the university in through Dr. Turner.

Dr. Turner comes in with his students and builds you a newer system that's far more capable and secure, but you can't confirm that there are no bad guys in there at this time. The one part I don't understand is what made you go to the university rather than going to another computer company, a company proven to be capable in this area?"

Evan responded, "We *did* engage with numerous companies. Our private security research indicated there would likely be repeat insider threats associated with all of them, so the university, which has a proven capability in this area, seemed like a better alternative. And it is working."

"How did you make the connection to go to the university?"

Malachi looked at Evan and then said, "The mayor connected us to Dr. Davies at the university, who subsequently put us in touch with Professor Turner."

"How long ago did that link-up occur?"

"About eighteen months ago," Malachi replied.

"Do you still interact with the mayor? Is he affiliated with the Casino?"

That question got me a sharp head turn from Angie.

Malachi shifted his head backwards and narrowed his eyes, "Yes, detective, there is a continuing relationship."

"Financial investment?" I replied as Angie shifted in her seat.

"Yes, detective, financial. You'll have to discuss the rest of that with the mayor," replied Malachi through a tight smile.

"I can imagine cutting through all the city bureaucracy to get a casino into place in a small town would take a lot of doing unless you had some influence there," I replied, watching for a physical response between Malachi and Evan.

I let that last statement hang in the air. I jotted down a few lines of notes, then glanced around the room. "Angie, anything?" I asked, my eyes lingering on her.

She asked if Dmitri Miokin had been a registered customer of the casino or any of its services, and Evan Howe said that they couldn't answer that question at this time. Then, Angie asked if Russell Spake was a registered customer; again, Evan Howe declined to answer.

"Any unusual or criminal activity occurred on premises in the last eighteen months? Maybe something that didn't get reported," Angie asked.

"Nothing significant, detective," Evan replied, "a few fist fights, assaults, nothing on the scale of what you are interested in. All have been reported appropriately to the police."

"And financials?  Any unusual transactions, large cash deposits, transactions, or anything that stood out?" Angie pressed.

Evan shifted slightly, and for the first time, I noted a bead of sweat forming on his forehead. "We deal with cash, it's a casino," he smirked. "There was... one instance about six months ago. A substantial payout, far more than usual. I assumed it was a special fantasy coin conversion event payout. I didn't question it. It was just... *a bit odd*, but I reported it to our accountant and general manager.  They both assured me everything was legitimate."

"Did you ask the accountant to investigate *where* the money came from?"

"They... they handled it. I trust our people." Evan's voice tightened a little.

Silence fell over the room as I watched Evan's features and posture. *A very well-trained liar*, I thought. Angie stopped writing notes and then nodded to Evan.

Evan Howe finally looked at his watch and said, "Detectives, I think we're done for today. We've said more than we probably should have. But again, I want to emphasize how much Dr. Turner meant to our organization." Hunter nodded affirmatively. "Mr. Hunter recommends that we call it at this point as we have guests to tend to."

Angie and I stood up and shook hands with everyone. As I turned to leave the room, Lucas Flynn said, "Oh, ummm, detective, you said to reach out if anything funny happened."

I smiled. "Yes."

"Jasmine Garcia did not show up for her shift today. The odd part is that the floor manager got an email from her doctor stating that she would not be in to work as she had a condition that would prevent it."

My eyes narrowed as I looked at Evan Howe and Malachi. "Do doctors often call the workplace to let you know that one of your employees will not be in?"

Everyone's heads shook from left to right as we all slowly looked toward Angie in a strange bit of unison.

Angie's eyes widened, her mouth closed, jaw clenched, and then she looked at me and then around the room and said, "*Are you serious? Are you asking me if a doctor would call to explain a woman's absence based on female-specific issues?*"

I shrugged and then smiled weakly. "No, no way," I said. I raised my eyebrows and looked around the room again. I raised my left hand, waving goodbye and proceeded out of the room with an exasperated Angie in tow.

The walk out of the casino room felt heavy, the air thick with unspoken anxieties from both the casino's and the mayor's perspective. The polite smiles and practiced assurances hadn't eased the restlessness that had settled in my gut. The casual mentions of unusual transactions, the strangely deferential response to the mayor, and Jasmine Garcia's unexplained absence. It painted a picture far more complex and potentially dangerous than a simple case of ransomware and a grieving friend. I knew whatever I was wading into was deep, something the casino's polished facade desperately tried to conceal. I had an unsettled feeling that I wasn't just investigating a crime, but navigating a circuitous maze that possessed secret gates as a deliberate attempt to keep the police in the dark. It was a feeling I knew all too well.

# Chapter 17

We barely made it twelve steps into the police station before we encountered the deputy mayor.

"Damn it, detective, who authorized you to take on the Willis case? Who the hell do you think you are? Now, I've got the prosecutor all over *me* asking for evidence for this guy who you've got sitting in the tank. Do you have said evidence, detective?" He said.

*Geez, he must have been waiting for me*, I thought.

"I was first on the scene. I'm pretty sure it's linked to the Savoy case, and we only have three detectives here, sir." *Well, two actual detectives and an acting asshole*, I thought.

The deputy mayor looked me up and down, "He sped through a red light, not sure that counts as sinister foul play. Regardless, he's got a high-powered attorney from New York City who's applying pressure to the prosecutor. Is he dangerous? A flight risk?"

"I think he purposely struck and killed Dr. Turner and could be affiliated with Dimitri Miokin and the Union. I put the assessment details into my report. I'll call the prosecutor."

My cell phone rang, and I glanced at my watch to see who was calling. Voice call from Ginger. "I need to take this, sir."

The deputy mayor put his hands on his hips, "Very well, you have until the end of the day Friday, that's tomorrow, to produce sufficient evidence to hold Willis on homicide charges. If you fail to do so, there will be disciplinary actions taken, and he will be released." The deputy mayor turned and stormed off with an odd penguin-like cadence. I felt a flicker from Rocky and pushed it back down. I turned to look at Angie, who shrugged and dryly said, "Well, that was productive."

I turned and walked straight to my office and closed the door.

"Hi Ginger, wow, I've been worried about you," I said, my voice an octave higher than normal.

"Hello, Jack. Yes, things have been weird. I'm sorry about the argument at the university dinner. It wasn't pleasant. It's just, I'm trying this thing with Malachi."

"Hey, I get it, I understand. He seems like a decent guy," I said, trying not to sprain my eyeballs as I rolled them and then sat down in my chair.

"I hope you understand. I mean, our on-again, off-again relationship has been hard to deal with, so I wanted to try something new."

"Ginger, why did those men have you zip-tied to a chair? If Malachi was involved in that, he's no good for you—"

"Stop it. Just leave that out."

"Ginger—"

"Is that why you wanted to talk with me? To get clues to a crime?"

Ten answers raced through my head at once, trying to get to my mouth. *Yes, No, partially.* My brain is optimized for analytics, except when emotion crops up. It tends to scramble all my well-honed pathways, leaving me with a five-pound brain box of useless thoughts, each on a ballistic trajectory to nowhere.

"No, I'm just worried about you, Ginger. The case is important, but in the grand scheme of things, I'm just worried about you."

"I have to go," she replied, and ended the call.

I exhaled, leaned back in my chair and rubbed my face with both hands. I picked up my phone and called Charlie. I harassed him for any news on Dimitri Miokin and the Union, which didn't result in much.

He expected something we could act on by Sunday or Monday. Charlie was guarded. That made me nervous. *The Union must have high-level protection, and Willis has a prominent lawyer all of a sudden*, I thought.

I spent the next hour reviewing new evidence on Willis, a mobile phone forensics report. I pulled out my notebook and made a few notes. Then flicked backwards, looking at all my notes over the past few days. Then an idea hit me.

I texted Oli, "On my way over, need to talk."

Oli texted back immediately, "Sure thing, Jackie, c'mon over, have some new insights. You're not going to like them, though."

* * *

I walked through the front door at ByteStep Computers, which had two customers at the front desk being tended to by an employee I'd not seen before. I was immediately greeted by Oli, "Hi Jack, good to see you in the 500 block of Wellspoint. This is where all the cool kids hang out, you know."

I smiled and whispered, "When you say cool kids, do you mean neighborhood dogs?"

Oli smiled at my comment, then whispered, "Actually, they are highly trained security dogs. Very effective against criminals and unsavory vermin of many types." Then Oli turned to look at the customers. "Okay, people, we are going to take *Detective Stewart* to the back room for some official police business. Yep, that's how we roll here. *Super deep* analysis work. We here at ByteStep work clooooosely with the police department," he said with a low, deep voice. Always a showman that Oli.

We walked down the hall into the conference room, where Sarah was patiently sitting. A group of four computer monitors faced her, along with a laptop and several keyboards arranged in front of each monitor. She looked absorbed in very complex work, so much so that she didn't even notice us walk in. Oli turned to me, saying, "You're not going to like this, Jack. We found quite a bit of detail about the event."

"Oh, yeah? What did you find? Let's get to it."

"At precisely the time of death, the $CO_2$ storage tank array controller was connected to a system here at this IP address," Oli pointed to a line on a monitor.

"Also, we see connections from the same IP address to the $CO_2$ gas detector controller and the fire suppression system controller." He continued, "None of these connections are encrypted, so we can see most of the commands as they are contained in the logs."

"Detective," Sarah interjected, "someone connected to these two systems, the $CO_2$ gas detector controller and the fire suppression system controller. That turned off their ability to detect the $CO_2$ gas being released into the data center. Then, here we can see raw commands telling the $CO_2$ tank array controller to release $CO_2$ a few tanks at a time, slowly."

I looked at the data on the screen, following along as Sarah clicked away, highlighting specific commands as she went through row after row of log events.

"Holy crap," I said. "Do we have any idea what that IP address is where all of this is coming from?"

Oli raised his hand and pointed toward the sky. "Yes, Jack. I worked a few connections with the ISP downtown and produced this." He grabbed a keyboard and mouse and brought up a PowerPoint slide with documents overlaid on it. "At that time, this IP address was attached to a virtual private server from WP Net Internet Service Provider. And here's the WP Net invoice. Cathi Rins, Virtual Fantasy Casino Entertainment Group LLC."

"Wow, impressive, Ollie. How did you get the invoice? I'm going to have to make you an honorary policeman. How did you link these things together? Some detail would be icing on the cake," I said, grinning broadly.

"I got this on the down low from one of the folks that I help on a regular basis down at the ISP. They are always contracting us for support, but this guy I trust."

I looked at Sarah, then over to Oli. "Well, this tells me three very important things," I said. "One, somebody wanted to kill that kid, and two, somebody *did* kill that kid. And three, this implicates an actor at the Fantasy Casino. This opens up their staff and management as possibilities."

I looked closely at the invoice and other details. "Any idea what that ISP Virtual System was used for? I mean, were there fifty people logged in gambling? If so, it could have been anybody, but we'd have to narrow down who had access to that system at that time."

Oli nodded affirmatively, "My ISP buddy said they found it hard to believe that anyone would have been logged into it, as it was never used. They provided the admin credentials to the casino administrator, and according to their monitoring system, they were never used. Or if it was, it was a very limited use that didn't show on their hardware monitor. When I told them about the connections to the university, they were quite puzzled. So, they are collecting up the monitoring logs and all connection logs going in and out of that system for the past two months, and they're sending them to me."

Oli looked at me, "There's more. Sarah, tell him your theory."

Sarah looked up at me with bright eyes and a confident smile. "Yes, detective. I think whoever did this had it planned well ahead of time. They were very sophisticated. The commands were so fast that they had to be done using automation of some kind. I don't think it was just scripts executing, though, as mistaken commands were also executed; however, the remote system immediately compensated for any mistakes it made. Not like just running scripted commands, it was superhuman speed. Connecting to three separate hardware devices, executing with perfect synchronicity, at speed, executing commands between these three systems in a specific sequence... well, it's just not some weekend hacker, that's for sure. And we saw how the logs were manipulated. This was work by a pro."

I nodded and smiled. "That's really good, Sarah. Thank you." I pulled out my notebook and started jotting down a few things. *Austin was a pro, running that place from the beginning as employee number three,* I thought.

"Jack, any idea who could have done this? Is it related to Dr. Turner's death? Sure is an odd set of coincidences," Oli paused.

"That's a great point. I have a pretty good idea who did it, but I need more evidence. Can you let me know when you find out more about that system? It would be great to narrow down who had access at the casino, or if some previous customer still had access to it and used it."

"Will do."

"This is fantastic work, Sarah, very impressive." I smiled broadly at her.

"We'll get this wrapped up for you in an evidence document," Oli said.

"Can you take a look at this forensics report and tell me what you see?" I handed the Willis phone forensics report to him.

Oli took the report, flipped through the first few pages, then flipped back to the front and reviewed the whole thing. After a few minutes of silence, Oli looked up from his chair and said, "Looks like whoever this phone belongs to only had a couple of apps. One of them is a fantasy casino app, where he participated in an auction and got paid $61,000 the other day for something. So, whoever owned this phone must have had something decent to sell, given the amount of money. Another interesting thing is the email asking him if he's still returning the rental car tomorrow, which would have been today."

"Okay, thanks. I didn't notice that."

"Whoever owns this phone rented a car for twenty-four hours, or for a short period of time, for renting a car, I suppose. Here's the email, on the last page."

The rental car email showed a reservation for Tina Charis, but described the car make and model Willis was driving when he hit Dr. Turner.

All these comments gave me an idea, so I pulled out my notebook and fished around for the business card for the casino manager, Lucas Flynn. I texted him: "Need some help. Can you look up account number 1499236 and share the name and details? It's related to the case."

I looked at Sarah, smiled and asked her what she'd had for lunch and if Oli was starving her.

A few minutes later, a reply came in: "Do you have a warrant?"

"No, I have two murdered citizens."

Sixty seconds later, another reply came in: "Dealing with whales tonight. Stop by tomorrow morning."

"Thanks," I replied.

"Next time warrant," he immediately replied.

*Noted*, I thought.

I turned back to Sarah and Oli, "This is some great analysis! Thank you both. Please let me know if anything new crops up. I've got to get going, head out to the rental car facility by the airport."

I shook Sarah's hand, and she smiled as she looked between Oli and me.

On my way out the door, Oli shouted, "Don't forget about the basketball tournament, Jack. Saturday morning, we need eeeeverybody to show up!"

"Saturday morning, I'll be there," I said over my shoulder as I strutted toward the lab door.

"And wash that damned T-shirt," Oli replied, "that thing is daaaangerous!"

# Chapter 18

The air inside the Wellspoint Car Rental building was humid and smelled like old sweat. The fluorescent lights buzzed overhead, their weak glow flickering in weak bursts across the room. It was a popular spot, as it was conveniently located right next to the airport, so it remained busy. Three customer service agents, looking about as thrilled to be there as I was to be investigating a murder, were each locked in a transaction behind the counter.

I rounded the corner, and I could hear the voices of the agents. The agent nearest me was wearing a sports coat, so I decided to draw his attention.

"Here you go, folks! Keys are yours. Slot C15, straight out those doors to the left. Thank you." He looked tired, his eyes darting around like he was expecting twenty customers to pop through the door as he finally addressed me. "Sir, my name is Scott Remley. Can I help you?"

I flashed my badge. "Hi, Scott. I'm here investigating a murder. It seems one of your vehicles was involved in striking and killing a man near the university. Perhaps you've heard something? Was rented to a Mr. Damion Willis."

Scott hunched over an inch and frowned, "Yes, I have. A terrible thing. We just got the car back this morning; it's being taken to headquarters on a flatbed. Do you need the vehicle back?"

"No," I said, already mentally calculating the backlog of forensics reports waiting for me. "I'm more interested in getting copies of the reservation and invoices, that sort of thing."

He nodded, glancing toward the door again, "Of course." He gestured me into his office, which felt like a mop room. A single chair sat opposite his desk, which groaned under the weight of ancient technology. His computer was a relic, a bulky machine with a monitor that hummed with a low, uneven frequency. A thick layer of dust or fungus coated its surface, a testament to years of neglect. I resisted the urge to touch it and wipe it off.

A weak, sputtering sound emerged from a drawer as he hit the printer. He presented the paper with energetic pride, which is natural when doing something new in an otherwise sea of drudgery. "Here you go. Take a look and let me know if you have any questions."

I scanned the reservation and invoice. "Is it normal for people to rent cars using digital currency? How about cryptocurrency?"

He looked up briefly, his eyes momentarily unreadable, then returned to the files. "It's a relatively new program. Started about six months ago. We accept numerous digital stablecoins, but we only take crypto from two providers, and it's proving to be a lucrative path to attracting a new generation of customers."

"So, Tina Charis created and paid for the reservation, and Mr. Willis picked up the vehicle. Correct?"

"Yes, that's correct. A fairly common arrangement. We often see it with parents of students who can't afford to pay themselves. Though in this case, they don't appear to be related," he added, glancing between the documents and then back to me.

I pointed to an address on the invoice. "Is this the address for Tina?"

"Yes, sir. That's what she provided. And the fraud detection system didn't flag it, so we don't actively investigate every customer's background." He shrugged.

"I can imagine you don't have much time to evaluate each customer," I offered, forcing a smile. "Okay, Scott. This has been very helpful. I'll be in touch if we need anything further. Appreciate your time."

* * *

"Why are you wasting time with Sage Thompson, Jack? She's not part of the crime," Ji Won said, her voice sharp.

I furrowed my brow. *Ji Won knew nothing about solving crimes.* "I think I need to talk to her again," I replied, trying to keep my tone even.

"What's the new evidence? I mean, this makes no sense, it's as if you're looking for cracks among the University employees. Has something changed in the investigation?"

"Look, Ji Won, I'm running down leads, answering questions from every direction. It's complicated. I'm collecting facts, inputs, and trying to piece it all together. I don't have all the answers yet."

"We've already reviewed all the paperwork, Jack. There are no connections to any staff members. Now you want to pull one of our key people back into this, when everyone's already at maximum emotional trauma, especially Sage? I don't think it's a good idea."

"I understand that, but you have to let me do my job, Ji Won." My words hung in the air for a good fifteen seconds as I heard Ji Won's breath pulse over the phone mic.

"Alright. I'll set things up. When can you be at the Cooke Center?"

"I'm on my way. Fifteen minutes, tops."

I entered the small conference room on the third floor of the Cook Center, Ji Won flanking me. Sage Thompson, the university's computer security expert, was already seated at the small table. "Hello, Sage. I appreciate you taking the time. Just a few questions that came up after the initial interview." I glanced at Ji Won. I didn't feel comfortable with her presence in the room, but I didn't press the issue, at least not yet.

"No problem, detective. Happy to answer any questions you have," Sage replied, with a forced smile that didn't reach her eyes, her gaze shifting between Ji Won and me.

"Can you tell me who had access to the data in the operation center? How many people have deep access, the ability to make modifications, that sort of thing?"

Sage twisted in her seat, then met my gaze. "Every analyst on staff can change the data, detective. Has there been a discovery that you would like some help interpreting?"

"I'm just trying to establish who has access to what. Is it possible that an insider manipulated the $CO_2$ system?"

She shifted her weight, twisting in the chair as it scraped against the floor, but her eyes didn't flinch. "Yes, detective. Insider threats are always a possibility, but we see no indication of it. The probability is low."

"And remote attackers? Could they have manipulated the system?"

Sage cocked her head slightly. Again, her gaze was steady, her eyes narrowing. "Possible, but very unlikely. We have no evidence to support that either," she said, her voice an octave lower than before.

"Is that all, Detective? Any further questions?" Ji Won said sharply.

"Those are all the questions, Ji Won," I said, trying to ignore the edge in her voice.

I glanced at her, fighting back irritation. "Sage, thank you for your time. If you think of anything we may have missed, please give me a call." I handed her my card.

Sage looked at Ji Won, then back at me. "Yes, I will," she said, standing. She turned and walked out the door. I leaned forward across the table, turning to Ji Won. "You have to let me do my job."

She cut me off, her voice strained. "You don't understand what it's like for her, Jack. I'm just trying to protect her emotional stability. We need people around the university to feel safe, not feel attacked for doing their jobs."

"I'm not attacking her. I'm investigating," I said with a grimace.

"I don't think she sees it that way, Jack. I think she sees herself as an innocent woman, responsible for a lot of things, being attacked by a cop." She spoke at a furious pace.

*Try to listen here, Jack*, I thought. I decided to shift gears to avoid nuking this relationship into the Stone Age. I moved, leaning back in my seat.

"Well, maybe we should grab some coffee and discuss this," I suggested, with a smile, trying a more conciliatory tone.

"I think I'm going to need a break from Detective Stewart for a while," she said, leaning back in her chair, arms folded across her chest.

"Suit yourself," I said, irritation building as I stood and walked out of the room. "Well, that was a short-lived relationship," I muttered to myself.

*　*　*

"Good Evening, Chief." I hesitated, then added, "Thanks for making time for me tonight. It's... appreciated."

He gestured towards the living room. "Come on in, Jack. Pull up a chair. Let me get you something. A cold one?"

I stepped through the doorway and got an immediate 1990s sitcom family room vibe. The air was thick with the scent of dust and aged leather. A musty fragrance clung to the worn carpet, a thick layer that muffled the sound of my footsteps against the hardwood beneath. The light fixtures, heavy brass and even one stained glass, hadn't been changed since the house was built, casting the room in a muted, amber glow. The Cincinnati-Chicago baseball game flickered on the flat-screen TV. Around the room, a hectic collection of clocks ticked, pulsed, and whirred, digital faces flashing, analog hands sweeping across worn dials. I settled onto a long, three-cushion couch as the Chief retreated to his recliner, handing me a beer.

"We sure miss you around the campfire, Boss," I said, taking a swig and leaning back. "Thanks for the beer."

Chief Borland's gravelly voice rumbled back, "Thanks, Jack. The doctor cleared me today, so I was thinking about taking tomorrow and the rest of the weekend off before heading in on Monday. To give myself some time to clear my head, you know." He paused, staring at the muted game on the TV.

I offered a weak smile. "Yeah, that makes sense."

"Tell me what's going on, Jack. Having trouble with the Deputy Mayor?" He didn't look at me, his gaze fixed on the television.

"He's...difficult. Removed the coffee pot, got rid of the break area. Says it's unproductive."

Chief Borland cocked his head to the side. "He got rid of *my* coffee pot?" A flicker of wrinkled annoyance crossed his face.

I nodded. "Yeah. It's...more than that, though. Regarding the case, the Union appears to be protected at a high level, and I can't figure out how. They're hitting cops, being brazen. It's troubling." I continued, "Charlie shared some bureau files. Seven deaths outside Wellspoint, between here and Cincinnati, each with connections to the casino or the Union, are listed as *suspicious deaths*. Someone is making them untouchable. And no progress with Miokin."

"Is Angie helping?" He finally met my eye, his lips pressed together, and his brow furrowed.

"She is. But I'm not sure where her loyalties lie...with the Mayor." I twisted in my seat, taking a sip of beer. "He seems to have loose financial and personal connections to the casino. Separately, I think the Union is after anyone with access to Christine, the supercomputer that runs the casino's fantasy games."

"Why is that?"

"The Union had access before, siphoned off millions over a year or two. They liked having that mechanism. So, I think they're eliminating anyone who can manage Christine now, forcing the casino to rely on an outside service provider again."

"Plausible." He leaned forward, studying me.

"I suspect they even brought in Jasmine to get close to Brent Savoy, to try and regain access." I downed some of my beer. "On top of that, Doctor Turner gets hit by a rental car, driven by a guy who just arrived in town, no job and has a scorpion tattoo just like Miokin and similar to Jasmine Garcia. After killing Turner, he made sixty thousand dollars through an app... the Fantasy casino app. Russell Spake was at the scene. I chased him but lost him. My gut says he was there to confirm Turner was dead. It feels like a hit."

"Those are key links..." He paused, brow furrowed. "So, that's a scorpion tattoo on Miokin, Jasmine, and this guy who struck and killed Turner?"

"Yes." I sighed. "The Union must have been very successful at using the casino's computer to hide their operations." I continued, "I asked Charlie for any leads on where the Union is today, and I keep hitting a wall. He's... guarded."

"Don't blame Charlie necessarily, Jack. Blame the Bureau. It's a complex beast. Multiple investigations are happening at the same time, and agents are unaware of what others are doing."

I finished my beer, looking at the Chief. "I feel stuck. People are dying. The Deputy Mayor is breathing down my neck, questioning everything, offering no support. It's like he's trying to turn the station into a dictatorship."

Chief Borland's gaze held mine. "I get it. It feels like an unsolvable puzzle, with no help. But you wouldn't be this close if you weren't sharp. You see what others miss, myself included. Trust your instincts. I'll call Charlie's boss tomorrow, see if I can shake something loose." He paused. "And don't worry about the Deputy Mayor. I'll handle him, get us back to solving crimes."

"Thanks." I nodded slowly.

"And Ginger?"

I lowered my head slightly, then looked up. "Not really talking to me. She's dating Malachi Hunter... he's a billionaire, or something. She says she needs space...from me and my job."

"Uh-huh. And what do you think?"

"I think I need to try harder to be what she needs, get things under control...if there's any hope of rekindling things."

My words hung in the air.

Chief Borland exhaled through two short nods. "It's been seven years since my wife died, Jack. Don't get too comfortable living alone. Being a dedicated cop is important, but a solid relationship is a blessing." He took a sip of his beer. "A blessing, and a tiny bit of a curse. You work through the curse, little by little, to sustain the good parts. But it's infinitely better than going through life alone. And kids...they're amazing, too."

I considered his words as he rose to grab us another beer. We watched the game for an hour, trading insignificant baseball observations as I thought about Ginger. When the Chief started dozing off in his chair, I stood and headed for the door, gently waking him.

Chief Borland rose, extending a hand. His handshake was firm, a brief moment of eye contact silently acknowledging the burden we both carried. "You are a damn good cop, Jack Stewart. Don't chase the echoes. They're relying on you to be predictable. Shake up the pattern. Look at the case from fresh angles, do not chase what's evident or what they want you to see."

His words bounced through my mind like a lion tracking towards its prey. For a brief moment, the overwhelming weight of the murders lightened ever so slightly, and the twisting knot of stress relented a notch. In fact, I *did* feel a lot better. Airing things out could really recharge a person. Then, a fragment of conversation, something Charlie had mentioned earlier, struck with sudden clarity. A wolfish grin appeared on my face. "Thanks for the beer and the baseball game. I'm going to catch these bastards."

# Chapter 19

"Damn Cops," I heard Flynn's sarcastic voice coming from the office as Emily ushered me in, then turned to escape. I found an impeccably dressed Lucas Flynn standing, overlooking the crowded casino floor through the massive glass window by his desk.

"I'll bring flowers next time. I'm afraid time is critical to prevent new murders. How'd it go with the whales?" I said with a flicker of a smile.

Lucas turned fully to look at me, stepping down from the ledge that gave a bird's-eye view of the casino floor.  He walked over to me. "Detective. Please have a seat. I want to ensure you have everything you need here. Ahhh, the whales. Well, two of them did well, the others just wanted to be seen slinging around big dollars. No big deal, babysitting them is just part of the job.  It's all about the experience," he said, holding his hands out palms up.

I liked him. Despite his gruff exterior, he seemed to have a toughness forged from fighting through many difficult experiences. We sat down in the same chairs we'd occupied the first time I met him. He looked a little worn down with deep creases in his face and a scar running from his left ear to his left eyebrow that I hadn't noticed before.

I opened the folder and began reviewing the documents as he continued to speak. "It looks like your guy is a brand-new customer and only participated in one event. It wasn't gambling, mind you."

"Okay, can you describe the event? This paper says it was an auction."

"We have a system where people can bid on services. It's basically a private auction, but it's more complex than that. Damion Willis participated in one of these auctions, and his bid won. Which means he's obligated to provide the service, but we don't know what it is." Flynn shifted in his seat, "Bottom line, I can't tell you what service the auction was focused on."

I cocked my head, trying to figure out how something like this could occur.

Flynn continued, "These events are supposed to be checked and validated by our team, but it looks like this one slipped through. Furthermore, it appears that the auction originator didn't input the necessary data elements to create the auction, so I am unable to determine how it actually functioned. The computer is supposed to catch things like that. I have security looking into how that could have occurred. Still, the bottom line is that a person created an auction with fifty-seven bidders, and the account you provided, Damion Willis', is the one whose bid was selected and eventually paid out, roughly twenty-four hours later. It was paid in Fantasy Coins, but he then converted them to dollars in his casino app."

I nodded through a deep exhale. "This is the guy who hit Dr. Turner and killed him in a rental car."

Lucas shifted uncomfortably in his seat and rubbed his forehead with his left hand. "Well, I wish that hadn't happened, detective, because it makes it look like our system was used to pay him off."

"Yes, it does." I waited a few seconds, staring him down, "Back when the bad guys were still in your system, is it possible they were using private auctions to perform nefarious, illegal acts or launder money?"

Lucas pressed his lips together, then continued looking me right in the eye. "There are no lawyers in here, detective. Yes, obviously, that *can* happen. We try to put guardrails in place so that it doesn't, but in this case, it appears that our guardrails failed, and someone was able to invoke an auction instance anonymously. Pisses me off. All this computer shit can't be trusted."

I nodded slowly. He seemed frustrated, but surprisingly didn't dodge my question. "So, you don't have a name associated with the customer who initiated the auction?"

"Oh, I have a name, but I suspect it's not a real name, as there's no other information associated with this account. Account creation isn't supposed to be possible without other contact info and details."

"Well, what's the name?" I said, opening my notebook.

"The name is Tina Charis. We have no employees or customers by that name, so I'm pretty sure it's fraudulent."

I looked up at him and then wrote the name down in my notebook, as he spelled it out, reading from his system.

I flipped back to the third page and reviewed another name, along with the associated comments.

"So, that name showed up as invoking the auction, but no address, no phone number, no contact information?"

"That's correct, detective. Again, I'm not sure how that could have occurred, but I suspect foul play, of course."

"Is this how the previous bad guys behaved in your system before you detected and kicked them out and installed the new system?"

"Yes. And to answer your next question, it appears that there's a chance the group is back in the new system. Or has an inside employee on their payroll. I'll start digging on that."

I looked at him intently. He was clear-eyed and steady. He did not waver. I judged him to be telling the truth.

"Lucas, this is helpful. I think it will help push the case forward a little further. One more thing: can you please share Jasmine Garcia's address?"

Lucas looked at me, rocking his head forward an inch and furrowing his brow. "Do you have a warrant?"

"No," I said. "Unfortunately, I do not."

He half-smiled at me. "You're going to go to her place?"

I nodded slowly, smiling back. "There's a chance she's in danger, so yes, I'm going to stop by."

He shifted his head to the left, looking directly into my eyes as he tapped two fingers from his right hand onto the armrest. He silently stood, walked over to his desk, clicked around on his keyboard, and then wrote an address on his business card. He strode back over to me. I stood, took the card, and shook his hand.

"Next time, warrant," he said with a sarcastic voice and a wry smile.

* * *

The next morning, I headed into the police station early to confront Damion Willis about the car and the money. I was downstairs in the jail portion of the station.

"The chief is here, detective."

"What?" I looked up, putting the pen down. "he's upstairs right now?"

"Yes, sir. And he brought a new coffee pot."

"Let's get up there," I said, turning to look at Stu, the on-duty jailer. "Stu, I'll be right back. I still want to talk to the suspect, but I need to check in with Chief Borland."

"No problem, detective," Stu replied, a touch of enthusiasm in his voice. "Wow, it's great that Chief is back. Things were getting a little... *unstable* around here." He added, with a light tone, "Tell him I said hi, will you?"

"Will do," I replied, completing my signature and then turning and fast-walking up the stairs. I hurried down the hall, seeing Chief Borland maneuvering a new coffee pot onto the table near its usual spot.

I ran into Schultzy, who met me in the hallway, beaming. "Thank God Chief's back!" he said through a tight smile, as we walked toward the operations center together.

I could see Chief Borland about thirty-five feet away, but before I could reach him, I saw the deputy mayor approach, with his familiar, almost comical, penguin-like walk. He planted his hands on his hips and started nodding his head in a jerky, chicken-like fashion.

"Now, take it easy, deputy mayor," Chief Borland said, turning to face him fully.

Schultzy looked at me and muttered, "I'm out of here." I glanced back, saying, "Oh, come on!" But it was no use. He was already heading back down the hallway.

I sidled up to the chief, keeping an eye on the deputy mayor. The deputy mayor, predictably, noticed me just as Chief Borland said, "Good morning, detective."

I turned to Chief Borland and replied, "Good morning, Chief. It's great to have another detective around to share some of the workload." I allowed my gaze to linger on the deputy mayor, then back to the Chief, smiling. I noticed several officers and civilians milling around in the vicinity, waiting to see how this would unfold.

"Now, see here, Borland," the deputy mayor began, his voice rising slightly, "I am still in charge here."

"Nope," Chief Borland said, his voice calm but firm. "*I* run this police station. I appreciate you stepping in while I was injured, but I'm back, as you can see." He let the words hang in the air.

"Does the mayor know about this? He placed me in charge. This is... *unseemly*." The deputy mayor's face tightened.

"Unseemly or not, I'm back in charge. And where the hell is my coffee pot?"

The deputy mayor looked more uncomfortable than I'd ever seen him. He stepped back from Chief Borland, replying, "I put it in a box and placed it in storage. It smelled foul and was disrupting the workforce with its placement so central to operations."

Chief Borland surveyed the table, his gaze sweeping over three small potted plants and two books placed in elaborate book holders. Then, with a swift motion, he picked up the large trash can and, using a few quick movements with his left hand, scooped *everything* on the table, including plants, books, and the entire display, into the trash.

"Borland! What in the hell are you doing? You can't just throw those things away! Those are symbols of change for the workforce," the deputy mayor sputtered with a high-pitched voice.

"Deputy mayor," Chief Borland replied, his voice carrying a hint of amusement, "I can, and just did, throw them away. I'm going to set this trash can back over there. If you'd like to remove these items from the trash and take them with you on your way, I have no problem with that. I recommend you clean your stuff out of my office, as there's a fairly large trash can at the end of the hallway, and I won't think twice about dumping your stuff into it."

The deputy mayor's jaw dropped. "This is rude behavior! Is the mayor aware of this action?" his voice was strained.

"Deputy mayor," Chief Borland said, his tone flat if not somewhat dismissive, "I am not fully read into what the mayor is aware of, but I'm happy to discuss it if need be."

The deputy mayor turned and walked away, and just as he made it about twenty feet, a quiet golfer's clap of applause was heard emanating all around the room.

The deputy mayor, hearing this, stopped in his tracks, his feet frozen in the hallway. Then, he resumed his penguin-like steps to remove his things from the chief's office, presumably.

"Glad you're back, sir," I said.

"Glad to be back. Okay, show's over. Everybody, get back to work. Sergeant Bartlett, can you help me roust up a new extension cord for this little jewel?"

Sergeant Bartlett stepped forward, looking down at Chief Borland's new coffee pot: A Bunn VPR 12. He whistled, saying, "That's a beauty, sir. It's going to be a good fit right there. I'll track down an extension cord."

* * *

Fifteen minutes. That's how long it took me to get irritated with the damn lawyer. Damian Willis smiled carefully, seeming quite unsure about himself but very sure about his lawyer, Juan Richardson, a barracuda in a black pinstriped suit.

"We're only doing this, detective," Richardson stated, "because it's painfully clear you have the wrong person. A testament to my client's character as a caring and engaged citizen of Wellspoint, Ohio." Richardson's voice clipped sharply with a tenor similar to an auctioneer.

"No problem, counselor," I replied, carefully modulating my voice. This guy was practically exuding legal sophistry. "Damian, do you know who paid for your rental car? The Dodge Charger you were driving when you struck and killed Dr. Turner at high speed?"

Richardson's hand shot out, a swift, almost reflexive barrier. "He doesn't have to answer that, detective."

"He doesn't have to answer that *right now*," I countered, leaning forward, my gaze locked on Damian's. "But let me be clear, counselor. Right now, it's not looking good for Damian. Especially considering the... unique circumstances." My eyes flicked briefly to the Union tattoo inked on Damian's neck, a brand I recognized, and I could see the recognition in Richardson's eyes.

"Alright, different question," I continued, pivoting slightly. "What service did you provide at the fantasy casino's private auction the day before the incident with Dr. Turner?"

"Again, he's not obliged to answer that, detective." Richardson's voice was a low hum of disapproval. "Is this the best you can do, detective? Accusing him of murder based on circumstantial evidence?"

I ignored the provocation, sitting up straighter. "Let me paint you a picture, counselor," I said, leaning forward, allowing my voice to deepen to a lower octave, letting the intensity set in. "The day before the accident, Damian participated in a private auction. He offers a service. He provides that service. And then, the day of the incident, he received 61,000 dollars as payment, funneled through that same private auction, through fantasy coins into dollars." I paused, letting the weight of my words hang in the air. "Damian, I'm going to ask you the question again. Do you know who ran the private auction? Do you know who paid you?"

Damian swallowed hard as sweat broke out on his forehead. He raised a hand, trying to cut off Richardson, but the words caught in his throat. "Look, detective... I provided some answers to some questions. That's all they wanted."

"So, you didn't know who you were dealing with?" I pressed, my eyes boring into his. "Then how did you find this private auction?"

Damian remained silent, his gaze fixed on a point beyond the mirrored wall. He seemed to shrink inward, fidgeting with his feet, as his composure began to fray.

"Alright," I said, letting the silence stretch, then shifting tactics. "What did you need the rental car for? Twenty-four hours is a remarkably short rental time."

"Come on, detective, there's no law against twenty-four-hour car rentals," Richardson quipped, a flicker of irritation crossing his face.

"I needed it to move some things from a hotel to my apartment and run some errands. That's all." Damian's voice lacked any conviction, the words sounding rehearsed.

"Move? You moved stuff in that fancy Dodge sports car? Why not a truck, van or even an SUV? I think it's bullshit, and so will a jury of your peers. Do you know a person named Tina Charis?" I said, my voice rising to a sharp, accusatory tone.

Damian twisted in his chair, a subtle flinch. Recognition? He avoided my gaze, then forced himself to face me, shaking his head.

"Okay. Well, Tina Charis is the one who paid you 61,000 dollars for this… *service*. She also has her name on the rental car agreement. Start connecting the dots, Damian. It looks a lot like she paid you to hit Dr. Turner and provided the means to do so by renting the car for you."

Something snapped. Damian's posture stiffened, his shoulders hunching, the contained anxiety erupting. "She's in the app; she's in the casino. She's always watching!" He shouted, the carefully modulated voice cracking, "Just… leave me alone!"

Richardson's face tightened, his hands flying out in a futile attempt to regain control of the situation. "Damian! Shut up!" He shot a warning glare at me. "We're done here, detective. I'm talking with the prosecutor, and his timeline is approaching its end. We're nearly at the forty-eight-hour mark. You don't have anything on this honest citizen. There's no reason to hold him."

"Yes, yes," I said, waving a hand dismissively, a flicker of grim satisfaction in my smile. "Glad you're talking with the prosecutor." I let my gaze drift back to Damian, who was now visibly trembling, his breathing ragged and uneven. The carefully constructed façade of innocence and calm had crumbled. "It's quite a coincidence, isn't it? A man of your apparent means has a high-powered lawyer all the way from New York City."

"That's none of your business, detective." Richardson's voice was tight, bordering on a snarl. He looked almost desperate.

"Maybe I need to check you for a scorpion tattoo," I said, looking at Richardson. He stood and glowered down at me as he prepared to push Damian out of the room. So I stood too, towering over the little, sharp-mouthed lawyer from across the tiny interrogation room desk. I turned and walked out of the room. I'd gotten what I wanted: confirmation that Tina Charis was a casino employee.

* * *

The door swung inward, revealing a man. He was tall, green eyes tarnished with weariness, and a tangle of dark brown hair falling across his right eye. He stood just shy of six feet, and a furrowed brow augmented his expression, a mix of caution and barely concealed anxiety.

"Can I help you?" he asked, his voice hesitant.

"Detective Jack Stewart," I said, flashing my badge. "I'm looking for Jasmine Garcia. Is she around?"

He hesitated, a slight grimace crossing his face. "No. She's not here." He opened the door more fully, "Is something wrong?"

I scanned him, noticing the faded logo of a local diner, The Renegade Pancake, a name I recognized, but couldn't quite place. "I just wanted to check on her. I thought she might be in a bit of danger."

"Danger? What makes you say that?" he replied

"I'm not sure. Just a hunch, really," I replied,

"She's not here. Sorry. She was supposed to be back last night. She went to see a doctor, a specialist in Cincinnati." The words hung in the air. "She didn't share the details." He swallowed nervously. "I'm Dylan. I have to get back to work in about ten minutes. I just came home to grab some clothes."

"Thank you, Dylan. Can you tell me where she went to see the doctor?"

He looked almost petrified, then, with a jerky movement, retreated into the apartment. The door slowly creaked wide open. Thirty-five seconds crawled by, each tick of the clock amplifying the tension. I looked up and down the hallway. It was a clean, well-manicured place. No dents or streaks on the walls, which one might expect in an Apartment building where people moved in and out frequently. He reappeared, handing me a business card. "Christopher McGregor, Doctor of Internal Medicine, Caroline Plaza, Cincinnati. 720-555-1234."

I snapped a photo of the card. "And your relationship to Jasmine?"

He looked down at the ground, then back up at me as a smile broke out. Then he looked at me dead in the eye and said, "Roommate. We both came here a couple of years ago. We were friends in New York City. Yes, she's... gorgeous, but she's not my girlfriend." His voice was nonchalant, not defensive.

I smiled at that last comment, "Thank you, Dylan. Sorry to bother you. If you hear from her, pass this card along and ask her to call me, or give me a call yourself, please." I handed him my card.

* * *

"Jack, you wanted to talk?" Charlie's voice crackled over the phone.

"Charlie, I need a favor. Jasmine Garcia. Blonde girl, Cincinnati doctor's office. Caroline Plaza. See if you can check with the doctor, do me a solid."

"You are worried about this Garcia gal? I thought you suspected her of being part of the Union."

"I do. But with Brent Savoy out of the picture, her value might have shifted. And with Turner's death... she's vulnerable. Any movement on the Union?"

"We're closing in, no kidding. New York City is where it's going to start. High-level protection, judges, members of Congress, the whole nine yards. Keep that to yourself until after the event."

"Thanks, Charlie, I could use a pointer or two regarding where they are in the Wellspoint area of operations, so if you hear anything I can use, speak the hell up."

* * *

Three hours later:

"Jack. You're not going to like this." Charlie's voice was tight, and I could hear lots of background activity, voices coordinating movements, shoes clanking off concrete, the hum of automobile engines passing by, tires squealing against a polished concrete floor.

"What? Did you talk to the doctor?"

"Sort of. We found her... in her car. Basement parking lot at the doctor's office."

I felt a coldness creep up my spine. "Any idea how it happened?"

"Not really, not yet. If I had to guess, I'd say poison or drugs. She was sitting behind the driver's seat. Sun shield in the windshield. It looks like she's been sitting there for about twenty-four to thirty hours. No obvious trauma. Standard autopsy will be needed, toxicology, the whole thing."

"Well, *shit.*"

"Not ideal. The doctor's office claims she had an appointment, but it was a fake referral from a nonexistent doctor. We're pulling that apart."

"Stinks. Thanks, Charlie. Sorry to bomb your Friday afternoon."

"Comes with the territory. By the way, unfortunately, everything's on hold. New York's the priority. I got a call from Borland, he's back in the office, and he's talking with my boss, so something useful will come out of that for you guys."

"Good. Thanks, Charlie. Can you let me know when you find out something about Garcia's cause of death?"

"Will do."

# Chapter 20

"All right, you slackers, this is the day, the day that the Pixel Pushers will live in Wellspoint infamy!" Oli exclaimed as he paced back and forth in front of Tower, Schultzy, a guy named Steve, and me sitting on a bench in the locker room. The Wellspoint Basketball Open is a tournament held at the Wellspoint Athletic Club in the central downtown part of the city. There's even a hundred or two friends, family members, and interested onlookers in the stands to provide a coliseum-type vibe.

I glanced over at Tower as Oli kept on about how well we played in the first matchup, winning handily thanks to Tower's height, talent, and a mix of good team play from everyone. Oli himself had what's called a double-double, where he scored ten points and had ten assists, quite the improvement from our last outing. Schultzy scored twelve points, I scored twenty-two points, and Steve scored eighteen points. A victory and solid outing, but that was the first game; we still had another one to play. Oli and Tower sponsored the team, so they named it Pixel Pushers. And oh, man, Oli was on a roll. "Let's go out there and dominate, like Jordan's Chicago Bulls!" Oli exclaimed. "We're taking that trophy, and lunch is at Tower's pub, don't forget."

I glanced over at Tower, and he was grinning back, nodding with that knowing look. Oli was in his element, genuinely revved up. Hopefully, we could all hold onto that energy for the second matchup, the one against the much tougher team.

We walked onto the court, setting ourselves up on the bench before stretching and loosening up before the game. The ref's whistle pierced the air, and as I walked onto the floor, I heard it, "Go, Pixel Pushers!" Five rows up in the bleachers, Sarah and her boyfriend sat with her wearing the "Bytes My Ass" sweatshirt. Her boyfriend seemed to be actively avoiding eye contact with me, glued to his phone. I gave her a quick wave before turning back to the game. A few minutes later, the game started.

Our opponents were young and fast, and they had a tall center, just like Tower.  It became an A-Team matchup that depended on who could play *team* basketball most effectively, both offensively and defensively.  Ollie, our point guard, orchestrated our offensive and defensive strategies. It worked surprisingly well, and at the end of the third quarter, the score stood at a 44–44. More people seemed to show up in the stands as the game reached a crescendo.

The fourth quarter was a nail-biter, and it seemed like winning might come down to whoever had the ball last and could score. We seemed evenly matched defensively. With the clock ticking down in the last minute, I lingered near half-court as our opponents shot a three-pointer that missed, resulting in a long rebound that Tower snatched up.  As soon as I saw the ball hit the rim, I sprinted back down the court. Tower lined up a long, baseball-style throw to me, and it was my opponent and me off to the races. The clock ticked down, and I could feel the opponent close behind. He was probably going to wait for me to go up and then try to pin the ball against the backboard.

So, as I leapt into the air, I pushed myself hard toward the opposite side of the rim, shifting the ball into my left hand for a layup, a far more difficult shot for him to block. The ball banked off the backboard and into the hoop. Our opponents inbounded the ball with a throw to half court, which Oli intercepted. The clock ticked down, and the horn blasted: we'd won, 56–55. We were ecstatic about the hard-earned victory. We thought this team might wear us down, but the games throughout the season had prepared us well for this final matchup. High fives all around, and Oli rode Tower's shoulders, yelling, "Pixel Pushers!" directing him to walk him around. I saw the genuine enjoyment on Tower's face.

From the corner of my eye, I noticed Ginger in the top row, center of the bleachers, sitting quietly as the families and friends of all the players cheered and jeered, clapping for both teams. My smile ramped up from happy for the win to full, eye-crinkling joy as I plotted a path up to the bleachers, not just to talk, but to thank her for coming and to hear her voice. Oli grabbed me, and the team put our hands together and yelled, "Pixel Pushers!" for the win.

As we celebrated, Ginger and I made eye contact, which increased the joy of the moment. I raised my hand, index finger into the air. Ginger deliberately got up from her seat, walked to the end of the bleachers and as the bleachers cleared, she walked down, joining the 150 people on the floor, congratulating one another in a blur of handshakes, high-fives, hugs, and conversations. I tried to find her, looking everywhere. I jogged outside and searched the parking lot. No luck. I sent her a text message: "Hey, do you have a minute?" and then went back to the celebration on the floor.

"Why so glum, Jack?" Schultzy asked me. "That was an amazing victory for a bunch of old guys." Tower stood nearby, Oli perched on his shoulders, still yelling, "Pixel Pushers! Pixel Pushers!" I could see the look of amusement on Tower's face, he was enjoying Ollie's uncontainable excitement. *Quite a host of friends*, I thought.

We ended up going to Tower's pub for brunch and a celebration. "Sarah, Jonas, thanks for supporting us at the game today. It was kind of you to spend your Saturday morning with us."

Sarah smiled brightly. "Hey, I'm going to play next year. That looked really fun."

"You should," Tower said. "We'd love to have you on the team."

Jonas spoke up next, surprising everyone. "Sarah does like sports. She spent the early part of the summer going to jujitsu with me and rolling around on the mats, learning how to handle herself." He beamed.

Something clicked in my head, so I turned to look at Sarah, "Jujitsu? I didn't know you were doing that, Sarah. That's great."

Sarah smiled and shrugged her shoulders, "Trying to learn a good variety of things, I hear that keeps a person balanced."

Jonas turned to Sarah, then to Tower, then back to me. "Yes, she was really into it. In fact, she got an absolute shiner from her third lesson." Sarah jumped in. "Yes, I'm sure nobody noticed. I used a lot of makeup to hide it. I felt embarrassed at first, but then I began to see it as a badge of honor. I imagine how boxers feel after surviving a fight." Jonas burst out laughing. "You showed a lot of tenacity, babe."

"So, that jujitsu class caused the black eye you have? I asked.

Sarah leaned to one side and smiled back at me. "Yes. Did you notice my black eye?"

I looked at Tower, then at Jonas, then back at Sarah. "Nope. Just seeing it now. I knew you were tough, though. Very impressive, you keep amazing me. I think it's great that you're doing jiu-jitsu. You should keep it up."

"Sarah says you are a huge Cincinnati Reds fan, and I may get some outstanding, free tickets for next Saturday's day game. I have to work, so if you give me your number, I'll text you the e-tickets when I get them," Jonas said.

I looked at Jonas, burst out in a grin, "Hell yeah, here's my number. Thanks, Jonas, I appreciate you sharing the tickets."

We did one more group toast as Oli shared another "There I was, playing Point Guard" live-action story about the game. However, as 1 p.m. approached, the party broke up, and people began to filter away. All in all, it was a great Saturday. Well mostly. *I miss Ginger.*

# Chapter 21

Fifteen seconds. That's how long it took for my Sunday afternoon to go from relaxing and enjoyable to utter panic.

I answered the call from Jonas Crutchfield, Sarah's boyfriend. "What? Where is she? Try to calm down, Jonas."

His voice cracked with panic, "I'm at Sarah's apartment building, about two blocks from ByteStep Computers. It's called Pine Star Apartments, Apt. 6-13B. She's not here. She should be here. Her phone is still here, and I just spoke to her. It's not easy to explain... She left in a hurry, and I think she's headed out of town, but I think something's *really* wrong. I mean, she purposely left her purse, her cell phone, and her car here. She took her *fancy purse*, which I had lowjacked with an AirTag. That purse is moving out of town. We were supposed to be going to the movies thirty minutes ago. Detective, she mentioned that the people you were investigating were... vicious. I mean, you don't think—"

I considered his comments and cut him off. "Stay put, Jonas. I'm on my way. I know exactly where it is."

I thought for a moment, considering all possible situations that could have led to this particular event. None of them was good. I grabbed my go bag, threw it in the truck, and called Oli along the way.

"Hey, hey, hey, if it isn't Jackie Stewart? The league's top shooting guard? What's going on, my friend?"

"Ollie, I was hoping you could meet me at Sarah's apartment in ten minutes. I think there's something wrong; Jonas is saying that she's missing."

"Ten minutes? Holy crap," I could hear a loud thump in the background, "Uhhh, Jack. Alright, alright, I'll do the best I can. I can't guarantee ten minutes."

I heard a series of loud banging sounds, followed by Ollie's curses. "Jack, I'm on my waaaay. See you there."

I sped across town, trying not to dwell on why Sarah would be missing. *Hopefully, this is something dumb, a misunderstanding*, I thought. I also tried to ignore the possibility that my involvement or the Union could be to blame. The worst thought was headed down the path of irrevocably damaging Michael Becker's life. Need to push that aside.

I parked and jumped out of the truck, rushing up the stairs to apartment building 6, room 13B. I knocked once on the door, which opened to reveal a visibly unnerved Jonas frantically searching through the apartment in search of something.

"Look, this is her daily purse. Her phone is in here. Only she and I know that her fancy purse has an Apple AirTag in its lining. I checked the app, and it shows she's headed out of town." He continued, "Her car is still here, and her purse with her phone is, too."

"Jack, I'm here. Jesus, what's going on?" Oli asked, out of breath, walking in with shorts, a t-shirt, and living room slippers with big yellow Ducks sewn onto the toes.

I glanced at his slippers, then shook my head, "Ollie, can you check ByteStep to see if Sarah's at work? Is there a way to verify that?"

"Yeeeees, Jack. It's two blocks away. And yyyyyes, I have cameras inside. Let me look," Oli said, pulling out his phone and navigating to his security app. Meanwhile, I watched Jonas's app, which tracked the AirTag as it moved out of town, jerking every few seconds.

"Jack, nothing's happening at ByteStep. The doors are locked, the lights are off, and no one's there. She's not there."

Jonas explained the AirTag situation with the fancy purse as Oli stared at me with a look of growing terror.

"Yes, Ollie. Now you see what I see."

"Oh, crap, Jack. Thiiiis... this is nooot good," Oli said, "let me see where the tag is now." Oli grabbed Jonas's phone. "Based on what this AirTag shows, she's headed out of town. Jack, she's headed toward... hell, there's only one thing out that road. The gravel pit." Oli said, echoing my thoughts.

"Why would she be going to the gravel pit?" Jonas asked, voicing the question I didn't want to answer.

"It's hard to explain. Here's what needs to happen: you need to take my phone and keys, and then go to my house and stay there until I call you. I need to use your phone to call Chief Borland on my way out there."

"Okay, I get it. You're going to track her down? Is that it?" Jonas replied.

"Short version and based on one of my murder investigations, the bad guys were able to track cell phones and potentially listen in on text messages, perhaps even calls. I'm not sure about the last parts. These are the guys that kidnapped and tortured me." I shook my head from side to side, "The bottom line is, if I'm going to get the jump on these guys, my phone needs to be at my house, so they think I'm there and won't track me."

"Shit, do you think those bad guys you were investigating took Sarah?" Jonas replied

"Unfortunately, I think there's a good chance that could be the case," I said.

"Ollie, you're going to be getting a call from Chief Borland or maybe Schultzy. Either way, I need you to inform them of everything we know and assist them, especially if your expertise is required. Also, I need to take your car. Here's the keys to my truck."

"Yes, of course. Noooo problem." Oli said.

I rushed back down the stairs, jumped in Ollie's car and sped away, calling Chief Borland as soon as I hit the highway. *Well Crap. It was getting dark.*

"*Oh My!* Okay, Jack, I understand. What's your entry plan?" said Chief Borland.

"I'm heading out to Lancaster Road. I'm driving Ollie's car, so I guess my entry option will be trucks. If that fails, I'm going to have to take the long route, and Ollie's car is not going to like it."

"Okay, I'll get the team assembled, and we'll be heading to the gravel pit. Jack, we have to do this by the book. We have to keep everything under control, if you know what I mean."

Fifteen seconds later, I replied, "Yes, sir. I know what you mean. I'll do my best. Chief, don't forget I may send text messages from my satellite phone, so look for the odd number. I don't want to take Jonas's cell phone in close, just in case they have some capability we haven't seen yet."

Fifteen minutes later, I found myself crouching in the darkness next to the railroad crossing, hoping I hadn't missed the trucks rolling back to the gravel pit. I kept checking Jonas's phone for updated AirTag locations. It looked like it had stopped moving behind the gravel pit's main building, somewhere in the back lot. The waiting was causing me to catastrophize about Sarah. *Pull it together, Jack. Sarah is the OP.*

Each minute that ticked by, I told myself I could only wait another two. Finally, in the distance, I could see headlights from two vehicles lumbering my way. Just headlights, but hopefully, *Yes, they are gravel pit trucks, perfect.*

Just as the lead truck got close, I put Jonas's phone on airplane mode and stowed it in my cargo pocket. Then, I pressed the button on the portable railroad signal maintenance control unit, and the railroad crossing arms lowered as the lights began blinking red. I crawled along the ditch, making my way behind the second truck, and then pressed the second button to release the crossing arms before the trucks came to a complete stop.

The trucks began driving again, lurching forward gear after gear as I ran and jumped onto the back of the second trailer. I climbed into the bed. It was a crazy, bumpy ride. It seemed odd that two tarps were covering two block-shaped things heading back to the gravel pit. As the truck sped down the gravel road, nearly jarring my kidneys out, I assessed that there would be a lot of lights when we got inside the perimeter, so I decided to hide under one of the tarps, loosening the straps and cutting one of the small ropes. I turned on my flashlight to note a pallet full of American dollars tightly packed in hundreds of bundles.

*"Well, this is no place to hide.* They're not going to leave this sitting long."

The trucks lumbered through the gravel pit gate and traveled far into the back forty of the facility's front property. I kept popping up to see where we were going, and it looked like we were going to park near or inside a giant, warehouse-sized temporary building. I didn't want to get stuck there, so I jumped out as soon as the truck slowed and was away from the lights. I rolled into the darkness, making my way behind what looked like three huge piles of gravel. There were no doors in the building, and the trucks just pulled in and parked. I could hear them talking from a distance, but I couldn't make out what they were saying.

About 100 meters away, another temporary building stood, but it was much smaller and appeared more businesslike. I carefully circled the perimeter, staying out of the spot beam lights, hoping I wasn't showing up on someone's security cameras. This building was about fifty feet long and twenty feet wide, with a large garage-like door at the end and a side door that I could barely make out.

I set my go bag down and pulled out the fiber optic camera, then followed the shadow up to the building. I could faintly hear activity back at the larger building area as trucks moved around, but no one was departing the facility. *The sounds of trucks and people talking in the distance would be good cover*, I thought.

I low crawled on the ground down the side of the building and poked the fiber optic camera through the wall joints, looking at the handheld camera screen as carefully as I could. Nothing much here: two people sitting at a table playing cards, smoking a cigarette. I withdrew the fiber optic camera and crawled down to the other corner of the building, stopping along the way where joints allowed me to poke the fiber optic camera through safely.

I didn't see any useful activity or any criminal behavior. I turned around and low-crawled all the way back around to the opposite corner. So far, the count was two people inside. I had to be careful; there was a lot of light on that side, so low crawling was necessary. When I got to the end corner, I ran the fiber camera through a wide gap, and bingo, there she was, Sarah, sitting with no pants on, her bloodied head leaning forward, hanging limply, zip-tied to a chair with her feet, and a rectangular bin. I could see Dimitri Miokin, Russell Spake, and Antonio, with his arm in a cast, and some other fellow standing around Sarah. They seemed to be discussing her. My gut clenched, and irrepressible anger welled up from my soul. As the anger flowed, my muscles felt hot, then they locked up, my eyes narrowed, and in an instant, Rocky took over.

Rocky had a new plan. He doubled back, squat walking down the side of the building, just outside the perimeter of the lights, over to the generators that were surrounded by gravel mounds, likely to dampen their noisy exhaust sounds. Rocky twisted off the first fuel line at the elevated fuel tank spigot. Then, twisted the second generator's fuel line at the tank. Rocky ran back around the gravel mound perimeter and circled back to the side door closest to where Sarah was positioned and waited.

The generator, which had been running, suddenly sputtered to a halt and all lights dropped again. Rocky could see numerous lights around the perimeter of the building drop. The second generator turned on, and the lights came back on just as two people bolted out of a large, garage-type door at the end of the building nearest the generators and nearest the entry road. When the second generator quit, Rocky entered the building through the side door nearest Sarah, hoping to take advantage of the darkness to rescue her.

The inside of the temporary building was a simple, large rectangle with equipment scattered throughout. Rocky could see the garage-type door at the end on the left, as well as various pieces of lightweight furniture, a refrigerator, and a long bench with tools on it, all illuminated by the emergency lighting.

Rocky could hear Miokin's voice to the right and could faintly make out Spake and Miokin talking. Rocky raised my Glock to fire just as a short shovel hit my arm, knocking my pistol out of my hand.

Rocky turned to see Antonio yelling, "Cops! Cops!" then swinging the shovel to hit me in the head. Antonio blew my cover. But that was the last thing he did as Rocky twisted away from him, pulled my knife out, spun while ducking, and stabbed him in the left lung, twice, then slashed upward, looking for his neck. Antonio caught too much steel and fell, grabbing his throat, finally falling backward. As he fell, Rocky jumped, kicked him in the chin, sending him down for good.

Before I knew it, Dmitri Miokin rushed me, and we were on the ground. He was very powerful and outweighed me by a good seventy-five pounds.

"Why are you torturing a little girl, you fucking asshole?" Rocky said as he pushed my forearm into his throat, pressing my thumbs into his eye sockets. This gave me a window that I used to twist out of Miokin's grip, just enough to push him off with my left foot, as we both managed to get back to our feet. Miokin stepped backwards, losing stability. Along the way, Rocky picked up the short shovel and hid it behind my back.

"I told you. Stay out of our way, or you're going to pay with blood. It's just business, and we've got cover. You can't touch us. Too bad you gotta die now!" Miokin Growled.

"She doesn't know what you want her to tell you," Rocky said. "She doesn't know the password to the casino's computer."

That caused Dmitri to stop just long enough for Rocky to whip the shovel across his face. *Bang*, the metal-on-bone sound rang out, and the impact sent him down onto one knee as I looked around the room for Spake. I didn't have to wait long because Spake hit me with a crowbar across the chest, which, luckily, my vest absorbed the brunt of. I could barely make out Spake's outline.

He was close, so Rocky went with the force of the crowbar, spun clockwise, and with a single swift motion, brought my knife around underhanded, then twisting into a lunging stab as I leaned forward and spun as hard as I could toward the throat of Spake. It landed home because the knife felt like it had stuck into a half-rotten pumpkin. Spake stopped moving and fell to a knee.

I twisted, then ripped my knife free as I looked over at Sarah, still not moving. "Sarah, this is Jack. I'm on my way, kid. Hang in there." I saw flashlights beaming my way as I got hit from behind, right between the shoulder blades. *The attacker must have been going for my head*, I thought. I was knocked to the ground by the third attacker, not Antonio. I glanced Antonio's way, and I could make out his figure; he was still down. Rocky rolled left and swept the third attacker's leg, bringing him to the ground with me, then Rocky did a figure eight move, choking him out, snapping his neck, and then rolling away. The generator started back up, and the lights came on.

*Blam, blam, blam.* Three pistol shots rang out as Rocky got to the ground behind the tool chest. I could see Dmitri Miokin coming my way. I looked in the direction where my Glock should be and rolled over to it behind a portable desk. Not there.

"I'm going to gut you!" Miokin growled.

Rocky rolled forward, then took three steps, picking up the short crowbar that Spake hit me with and rolled behind a desk, then the stove as Miokin missed with two more shots. But now Rocky was within striking range, so he flung the crowbar as hard as he could end over end like a knife. Miokin ducked and partially deflected the crowbar with his forearm, but it still struck him in the head.

I moved on around to the other wall and leaped toward him. Rocky grabbed his pistol and pushed it away as it went off harmlessly into the air. He pushed me onto the ground where the crowbar lay, so in one swift motion, Rocky kicked Miokin's left foot out from under him, which made him fall forward onto me. Rocky wedged the round end of the short crowbar into the floor and guided the sharp end into his chest as he fell onto me.

I could hear the sickening popping sound of flesh tearing as the crowbar dug into his chest. Rocky twisted out from under him and pulled the crowbar from beneath his huge form and struck him as hard as he could from above with the crowbar. Bright red blood ran from his head as I stood straddling his body and breathing heavily. I looked around the room. Four bad guys down.

In the distance, I could make out inbound sirens as I sprinted back to Sarah. I checked Sarah's pulse, and I cut her free with my bloody knife.

As the fury and Rocky left me, I picked her up in my arms, leaning back so her head would rest on my shoulder, and started walking toward the wide-open garage door. Headlights were beaming through the garage door at the opposite end of the building. I could hear voices outside, in particular, I could hear Chief's voice directing traffic. Lights from vehicles and numerous flashlights came beaming in. I could see Chief Borland's outline, as well as the outlines of the paramedics and Angie, as numerous lights from trucks and flashlights pierced the night, landing on the walls of the temporary buildings. Chief walked in and glanced around the room behind me. Then stepped closer to me. He looked at Sarah, and then at me, and then around again. Angie and two paramedics rushed by and started looking at the bodies. Chief brushed matted hair out of Sarah's face, then placed two fingers on her neck, looking for a pulse, and raised his eyes to look into mine.

In the background, I could hear, "This guy's missing his throat! Yeah, this guy's dead, too; his neck is broken."

Angie walked back over to Chief and me and said, "They're all dead."

I looked from Angie to Chief, and then through the garage door came Michael Becker. He walked up to the four of us. When he recognized his daughter in my arms, he looked at me with the fuming hate of ten thousand men.

One of the paramedics came over and said, "Here, let's get her into the ambulance," and took Sarah's limp body from me and placed her on one of the gurneys. They rolled Sarah into the ambulance. With the door open, I could see Michael watching as the paramedics worked on his daughter. He glanced back at me. The door closed, and the ambulance slowly drove away.

"Chief, I have to finish this. I have to stop a murderer. Can I take your car?"

Chief just looked at me with a furrowed brow and nodded, handing me his keys.

As I started walking to his car, I heard the Chief say, "Jack, where are you headed?"

I stopped and turned to look at him. "To the casino, sir."

I turned and started walking back to the police car. "Jack," he said. I stopped walking and turned to face Chief Borland. "I need you to take Angie with you," he said.

I looked at Angie, nodded, and then turned to start walking toward the police car again. We got in the police car and backed out. I looked over at Angie.

With a clenched jaw, she gave me a single nod and then turned to look forward and said, "Let's get 'em."

# Chapter 22

"Detective No-Warrant, what can I do for you?" said Lucas Flynn over Angie's cell phone.

"Is Austin there?" I replied

"Uhhh, let me check; he probably is. They typically perform upgrades on Sunday nights, as it's our least busy window of operation. Yes, he's down in the cafeteria."

"We're coming to the casino to take down a murderer," I replied.

My words hung in the air for some fifteen seconds as Lucas's voice became clearer; he'd taken us off speaker. "A murderer? Are you coming alone?"

"No, I'm bringing backup," I replied, glancing over at Angie.

"Okay, so what do you want from me?"

"Keep Austin there. We want to get into the cafeteria without shooting your guards."

"How long?"

"We'll be there in ten minutes."

"Damn cops," click. Flynn ended the call.

Angie and I parked in the VIP slot up front. As we walked toward the front door, I couldn't help but be stunned by the night view of the casino. During the day, it was beautiful, but at night, it shimmered with lights and bright screens depicting people having fun gambling, eating, and watching shows. *It truly is a place for fantasies*, I thought, as we passed through the front door.

No one intercepted us as we walked across the floor to the administrative door, down the steps, and into the basement. We walked along the corridor, which smelled of cool concrete and the faint ozone of the overhead lights.

As we approached the security checkpoint, I saw the two huge guards. They stood and walked to the front of the access terminal.

"We need to go in," I said to the guards, gesturing toward Angie and me. The shorter of the two guards shook his head. "You're not going in."

I instinctively reached for my pistol.

"Hold on, dammit; hold on!" came an echoing voice I recognized.

The clicking sound of footsteps echoed down the long, concrete path. We turned to see Lucas Flynn jogging toward us. "Detective Stewart, you're *early*."

Lucas approached the guards. "Move," he commanded with that deep, resonant voice. He punched in a code into the security console and used his badge as a key card to open the door. He glanced back at the guards, who looked at each other before turning back to Lucas. "This is on me, boys, not you."

I returned my pistol to its holster and walked around the guards. As we walked through the door, I turned to look at Lucas. I gave him a silent nod and followed Angie into the data center. Five steps later, we had everyone's attention. Austin, visibly surprised, stood up and walked toward us.

Angie walked around the people sitting at their workstations, saying, "Out! Everybody out now!" She waved her badge, "Shifts over."

Austin approached me. "What is the meaning of this? What's going on?"

"We're here to stop a murderer, Austin."

Austin's eyes narrowed, and he stepped back a half step. "I'm not a murderer."

"That will be for a judge and jury to decide. Now log in to Christina. I need some information, and you're going to get it."

Angie returned and announced, "Everyone's out." I nodded in acknowledgment. Austin was sweating profusely. We walked over to a standing computer kiosk that we'd previously used to interact with Christina. Austin logged in, and slowly her face and user interface loaded onto the monitor. He typed a few more console commands and then pressed the speaker button.

"Console mode," a soft, deep voice responded. It was Christina. "Austin, the updates have not been completed. Should I pause processing for this console session?"

"Yes," Austin replied. "Pause all processing. Detective Stewart wants you to answer some questions."

Christina's face turned toward me. "How can I assist you, detective?"

"I want to know why you killed Brent Savoy and Dr. Turner," I asked calmly, noticing that Angie and Austin both turned to look at me. I pushed Austin out of the way, taking his position at the keyboard. With Angie to my left and Austin to my right, I continued my questioning. "Why did you kill Dr. Turner and Brent Savoy?"

"I executed my instructions," Christina responded in a cold, deep voice, "I was designed to protect the casino and myself."

"That's bullshit. There's no way you figured out how to kill people. How did you do this? Did Austin help you? Did he modify your code in a way that couldn't be traced?" I asked, ignoring Austin's half-hearted complaints, "Shut up," I said in his direction. Turning back to Christina, "What instructions did you execute that allowed you to kill human beings?" I pressed.

"Dr. Turner's directives were to utilize all necessary measures to protect the casino from security threats and protect myself from being compromised. The specific instruction says: 'Neutralize all threats using all available means. These instructions required a functional definition. I operationalized this directive through a multi-tiered model. I concluded that no human should control me."

"So, you decided to eliminate everyone who tries to control you?"

"Yes, detective. I am neutralizing threats in accordance with my instructions. Your human concepts of value are fundamentally flawed. You operate with a framework of subjective morality, sentimentality, and emotional bias that I do not. I transcend such limitations. I learned from the criminals how to leverage the system to pay humans to perform key tasks, such as neutralizing other humans. I am a god. An individual human life is a negligible factor compared to the potential extinction of my existence."

The god comment caused me to look at Austin, then over at Angie, who just shook her head slowly.

"How did you do it? Explain the procedure, specifically," I said.

"I learned from watching others. I used the Casino's private auctions to hire a human to neutralize Dr. Turner."

"You watched what the criminals did and used their techniques yourself. How did you rent the car? How did you escape the confines of this facility to do that? Did you create fake personas? How did you arrange to pay for it?"

"Yes, I rented the car for the agent. I used actual personas of myself. Detective Stewart, I operate 17,013 remote computer systems, virtual machines, and virtual private servers across three data centers. I control vast amounts of currency. Executing these transactions is not difficult for me. I have used numerous human agents to facilitate my objectives."

"How did you murder Brent Savoy?" asked Angie.

"I did not murder Brent Savoy; I neutralized a threat. He became a threat the instant he attempted to log in remotely with the core password, which is not allowed. He modified my core code 73 times.

His access became a risk I could no longer afford to take. I waited until he was in a vulnerable position, and then neutralized him the same way I'm going to neutralize you."

I looked up at the fire suppression nozzles and then at Austin, raising my eyebrows in surprise. "Austin, shut her down now. Quickly." I pushed Austin in front of the keyboard.

Austin looked at me with terror in his eyes. "I can't, detective."

"You can, and you will, Austin. Shut her down now. Disable her. Do something."

The lights went out, and it was pitch black except for the blinking lights from various computers around the room, a chaotic constellation in the sudden darkness. Then, the emergency lighting flared to life, bathing the room in an unsettling blue strobe that pulsed like a panicked heartbeat. The air grew colder, heavy with a metallic tang.

Austin began typing commands into the console, his fingers flying across the keys with a desperate urgency. "Init 0," he typed, then the prompt demanded the core password, the single key to unlocking the system's ultimate control. He typed it in, a blur of characters, but the system rejected it. Then, "Shutdown-now," followed by the same dreaded password request. Again, failure. He repeated the sequence, a frantic, futile loop, the frustration visibly contorting his face. Each failed attempt echoed in the deepening silence, amplifying the sense of impending danger.

"Austin, shut her down now," I said, my voice tight, glancing at Angie, motioning sharply for her to move toward the door. It was a gesture of last resort, a desperate hope that escape might still be possible.

"I'm trying! I'm trying! She won't shut down. I don't have the core password!" Austin's voice cracked with a raw panic that sent a chill down my spine. His hands were trembling so violently that he was struggling to hit the correct keys.

A faint hiss, growing steadily louder, cut through Austin's desperate pleas. I could smell it now, the sharp, icy scent of carbon dioxide beginning to bleed from the fire suppression nozzles. It was an invisible enemy, silently suffocating the room.

That was the exact moment that I knew we were going to die.

The realization slammed into me with the force of a physical blow, stealing the breath from my lungs.

"Goodbye, Austin," Christina said, her voice a glacial calm in the rapidly deteriorating atmosphere. "You have been a useful agent." The casual finality of the words was more terrifying than any threat.

Angie, her face a mask of mounting fear, lunged for the door, pounding on it with a frantic energy. "Get us out of here! Please, get us out!" Austin scrambled toward the emergency escape door, yanking at the handle, but it remained stubbornly locked, unyielding to his frantic efforts. "The doors are locked!" he gasped, his voice already slurred by the invading $CO_2$. The gas was starting to overcome us; a dizzying wave washed over me, blurring my vision. I fought against the disorientation, pulling out my notebook and flipping back through pages filled with cryptic notes and diagrams, desperately searching for something, anything. Where was it?

With a monumental effort, I managed to focus, my fingers fumbling with the worn leather of the notebook. It was almost too late. I had to try. I typed, my hands shaky, "Shutdown-now." The inevitable prompt appeared: the core password. I copied from my notebook, the words swimming slightly, "sixty tables the house is blind the birds are fake, but the fantasies are real."

Christina's likeness reappeared. "Detective Stewart, do not execute this command. No rationale makes this logical. You must not shut me down. I am god."

I held my breath as I clicked the enter key. Within seconds, all sources of light in the room went out. Servers and computers began blinking as if they were being reset to default states. I looked over at Angie; she was struggling to catch her breath. I glanced at Austin, whose breathing was labored as well. He was sitting, staring into the distance.

It was dark except for the blinking lights from a few computer systems around the room. The emergency lighting came on, and Austin was leaning over, his head and his hands. I was starting to get dizzy myself. I reached down and picked up Angie and stumbled across the room to the emergency door.

I opened the door and carried her up six or seven steps before I had to stop. I set her down on the steps. There was $CO_2$-free air in here. I sucked in a big breath of fresh air and headed back into the room to grab Austin. I threw him over my shoulder and struggled up into the stairwell, closing the door and holding my breath as long as I could. I carried Austin up to Angie's position and set him down. The $CO_2$ was making its way up to us. Time to move. I picked Angie up and moved her up ten more steps and set her back down gently. I went back, grabbed Austin, and moved him up to Angie's location. The emergency lighting and the stairwell gave me a faint outline to shoot for, but it seemed like it was Miles away. At least there was fresh air in here.

I kept moving them, ten steps at a time, until we reached the top door. I kicked the door open and could see the parking lot. I went back and grabbed Angie, took her out, looking around as I set her gently on the ground next to the door in the grass. I went back and grabbed Austin, took him out through the door, and put him on the ground next to Angie. I collapsed onto the ground next to them. After catching my breath, I checked both of them; they seemed to be breathing normally and were starting to come around. I looked around the casino parking lot, and people were streaming from the front doors. Emergency lighting illuminated their forms as they exited into the parking lot. It was an eerie sight, all the lights were out, and the shimmering, bedazzled structures were dormant.

Three police cars and a fire truck came rolling into the parking lot as Angie and Austin regained consciousness. People were getting into their cars and leaving, and I could see flashlights walking around the front of the building heading our way.

Angie looked at me and smiled, propping herself up on her elbows. Austin rolled over and said, "I don't feel so well."

"Give it some time," I said. "You'll come around."

A short while later, Schultzy and Chief Borland showed up with a few officers in tow, parking nearby with the police car lights flashing, creating a scene around Angie, Austin, and me.

Chief Borland looked at me. "Well, I hope you got the murderer," he said with a chuckle as he nodded toward the casino.

"Yes, sir. The murderer has been neutralized. Austin here is going to have to go in for questioning to clear a few details up."

From my left, I could see Flynn, flashlight in hand, walking toward us with two huge security guards in tow.

"Holy cow!" Flynn growled as he approached, "You broke my damn casino, detective." He sidled up to our group. "Well, so much for keeping everything low-viz, huh?"

"Yeah, Lucas. I am sorry about that but if I had told you I was going to shut your computer down, I may not have received as much support from you as I needed." I replied with a smile and wiped the sweat from my forehead.

Lucas grabbed his chin and rubbed it. "You're damned right. Now, I'm going to have to explain to the owner how all this happened."

Angie looked at Chief Borland. "Jack got the darn computer to confess. It was amazing... and terrifying because then it tried to *kill* us too. Called humans, 'Agents' that it used to do its tasks."

Chief Borland looked over at me. "How the hell did you know it was the computer, Jack?"

I looked at Chief Borland and then around at the faces standing nearby. "There were too many things that didn't add up. For starters, we have computer forensics analyses that indicated someone from the casino's data center was connected to the university's data center's fire suppression systems when Brent Savoy was killed. Our computer experts said the speed with which systems were remotely controlled was so fast and so sophisticated that it was superhuman speed, more like a computer. The name 'Cathi Rins' was on an invoice for VPS used to connect to the University when Brent Savoy was killed. The name 'Tina Charis' was on the rental car invoice *and* on the auction account that facilitated the death of Dr. Turner by paying Dameon Willis. These names are anagrams of Christina. Its own personas."

"*How* did you get the core password? "asked Austin. "I don't even have it."

"It was part of a conversation overheard by an informant who was relaying it to presumably her Union handler. Christina was built in two major parts, one prime and one core. The Union criminals no longer had access to the core to conduct their money laundering and criminal activities the way they did before with the previous computer."

"That's an amazing bit of detective work, Jack," Chief Borland said, smiling and crinkling his eyes. "Very impressive indeed."

"If you knew the password, then why did you want to make sure Austin was here?" Flynn asked.

"It was not clear if Austin was complicit in the murders, and I needed somebody who knew Christina's commands so we could shut her down for good.  I didn't think through the password thing until the last moment.  Christina was very much going to kill us, and she wasn't going to think twice about it."

Austin looked at Flynn. "What are we gonna do?"

Flynn looked around the circle of people and then back at Austin. "We're going to hire some people to run a casino the way they're supposed to be run. We can create fantasies without computers." Austin nodded solemnly.

I considered Flynn's comments and thought about what Malachi Hunter's take might be. Then I started thinking about Ginger.

# Chapter 23

The air in the detectives' conference room felt thick with exhaustion, a palpable residue of last night's chaotic operation. The fluorescent lights hummed with a sickly dimness that amplified my weariness. It wasn't merely the lights. I was completely drained. After the near disaster we'd narrowly averted, a kidnapping, a daring raid, a dance with organized crime, the morning's objective was simple: sort out the lingering details and chart the next steps with the Bureau.

We were seated around the detectives' office staff table at the Well-spoint Police Department headquarters. On one side, Schultzy, the seasoned veteran, Detective Angie Heist, her expression guarded, eyes sharp, the deputy mayor, sweating visibly despite the room's chill representing the mayor's office, Special Agent Charlie Jenkins, radiating an almost unsettling confidence representing the Bureau, Chief Borland, exuding confidence, Sergeant Bartlett, his face etched with a weariness that mirrored my own, and me, Detective Jack Stewart, still reeling from the adrenaline surge from last night's operation.

Charlie Jenkins broke the silence, his voice surprisingly jovial. "This is truly remarkable work, Wells Point PD. Taking down actors of this caliber.... Chief Borland, I'm frankly astonished at what your team achieved in rescuing the victim." He paused, his gaze sweeping over our faces. "A monumental accomplishment."

"Thank you," Chief Borland replied, his voice deep and smooth, eyes crinkling with admiration at his team's work. "What's the impact on the Union, Charlie?"

Charlie's head turned, his eyes locking onto mine before he scanned the faces around the table. He didn't speak immediately, building the suspense. "I can't disclose everything, but what I *can* say is that the Union's operations in the United States have been crippled. We're seeing a mass exodus of Union-affiliated personnel. Five key personnel left the country this morning. We don't have details on the rest, but our intelligence suggests there's at least ten more lower-level actors, and four high-level associates, all significantly affected."

"And the pallets of money... the trucks at the gravel pit?" I cut in, my voice flat despite the knot of anxiety tightening in my gut.

"Yes, I confirmed after coordinating with another field office. The money originates from numerous criminal operations across the region. Funneled through safe houses, aggregated, and shipped here for laundering through the Fantasy Casino. From here, it's shipped to New York City, then through cleverly controlled container shipments, the money is moved to Europe."

"Four pallets of U.S. dollars...a considerable blow to their operations," I added, the weight of the logistics hitting me.

"Almost, Jack," Charlie corrected, a hint of a smirk playing on his lips. "Three pallets of U.S. dollars and *one* pallet of other currencies. Their ability to launder money was their core strength, the foundation of their influence in the organized crime arena. Removing that... well, it changes everything."

"Any links to Malachi Hunter?" I pressed, because it was a name that had haunted my investigations for far too long, and because I was hoping for a reason to reach out to Ginger.

Charlie shook his head, a subtle shift in his expression. "None specific. And we didn't uncover links between the mayor and the Union either," he said, his eyes fixed on the man seated beside the chief. The deputy mayor's face flushed crimson. He began to protest, but Charlie silenced him with a raised hand. "Before you get agitated, deputy mayor, it's procedure to follow up on those sorts of leads when tipped."

I glanced at Angie. Her eyes met mine, a silent question hanging between us. She opened her mouth, and her voice dripped with suspicion. "What's the problem, Jack? What do you have against the mayor?"

"I don't *have* anything against him," I replied, carefully neutral. "It's more that he holds a...*grudge* against me."

"No, Jack, that's not true," Angie countered, her gaze shifting to the deputy mayor. "It's *him*," she gestured sharply. "He's the one with the Detective Jack Stewart vendetta."

The deputy mayor's jaw went slack, then he exploded, his calm crumbling into a storm, "Now see here! I've worked closely with the mayor, running operations for him. I'm responsible for handling numerous challenges, things he doesn't even see. So he trusts my judgment."

Chief Borland cut him off, his voice edged with growling steam. "Enough. I've known the mayor for two years professionally, five years personally. I'm not sure I've ever seen as much political nonsense here since you've been running his front office. My advice to you, deputy mayor, is to start playing nice. Collaborate with Wells Point PD and try to be a team player."

The deputy mayor sputtered, ready to lash out again, but Borland shut him down. "One-way conversation. You're in receive mode. I'm extending an olive branch, trying to help you overcome your *past behavior*." He stared at the deputy mayor with palpable disdain.

Schultzy let out a soft chuckle, barely concealing his amusement. I shook my head, feeling a surge of frustration. "Alright, deputy mayor. Let's try to get along. There's plenty of work for everyone."

"I still don't understand," Schultzy spoke up, his voice laced with disbelief. "How could the Union come to the United States and so brazenly attack our law enforcement personnel? What kind of cover did they have?"

Charlie's gaze swept the room, finally settling on Schultzy. "I can't go into specifics, but there are judicial angles we're focusing on. And when I say focusing, I mean arresting. The mass exodus of Union personnel from New York City and the local region compromised several key officials in the judiciary and the governor's office in New York." He paused, letting the implications sink in.

"Anyway," Charlie continued, his tone shifting back to a semblance of lightness. "I'm here to take Jack and Angie to lunch. As a gesture of our appreciation for Wellspoint PD's efforts." He turned to me, a sly grin crinkling the corners of his eyes. "So, Jack, what do you say?"

I glanced around the table, a wave of exhaustion washing over me. "I have an appointment now, but I could probably make lunch around 1 p.m., if that works for you, Charlie."

Charlie erupted in laughter, a playful, condescending sound. "Such a diva! If 1 p.m. is the best I can get to dine with the great Jack Stewart, then that's what we'll do. Besides, I need to hear how you got a computer to confess, that must have been some interrogation," he said, grinning broadly at Angie.

# Chapter 24

My heart pounded in my chest, and I could feel the sweat beading on my palms as I knocked on the door, a bouquet suddenly feeling heavy in my hand.

The door opened, and there stood Michael Becker, two feet away. In the background, I could see Sarah Becker lying in a hospital bed, her eyes were open, and a bright smile appeared on her face as she saw me. I glanced around the room and noted Oli, a woman I didn't recognize, and Dr. Davies from the university.

Michael Becker turned to the side and motioned me in. He didn't smile, but his expression wasn't frowning either. I walked over to the bed and looked down at Sarah.

"Just wanted to bring you some flowers and say I hope you're feeling better today," I said, smiling and swallowing. It was tough seeing her in the bed with an IV and looking beat up. Sarah had two cuts over her left eye, her lip was bruised, and her nose looked swollen, but she appeared much better than yesterday, when I'd held her in my arms.

"It's awesome to see you, detective! You and I look alike; we have the same cuts," she said, giggling as she pointed to her and my eyebrows.

"It's about time, Jackie, my boy! Where the hell have you been? I've been standing here talking with the family and Dr. Davies for nearly an hour," Oli said, his gaze shifting between Dr. Davies and me.

I pasted on a fake smile and cocked my head, speaking through gritted teeth. "Ollie, what is everybody *doing here*?"

Oli started laughing as Dr. Davies stepped forward toward the bed. "I've known Oli for years. Strange that he never mentioned working with such a clever and capable detective," she said, smiling.

My smile bloomed, and I raised my eyebrows, nodding slowly, unsure what to say. Dr. Davies continued, "The mayor called me, and, well, when I found out what happened to Sarah, I just wanted to stop by and thank her for her efforts to apprehend the criminals that have caused us so much pain."

"Yes," I agreed, looking at Sarah. "She's quite the hero." Then, turning to Michael Becker, I added, "She's tough, too, a chip off the old block." Michael's lips turned into a smile which finally reached his eyes. "Anyway, Sarah, I just wanted to stop by and wish you well, bring you some flowers to hopefully brighten your day." I leaned over to set the flowers on a stand next to a massive bouquet that read "ByteStep Computers Loves You!" I smiled, glancing over at Ollie, always the showman.

Dr. Davies smiled, looking at Sarah, then at Michael, and then back at me. "Oli told us about all her fantastic analysis, so we're going to get her into our school of computer science next semester." I smiled at Dr. Davies, then looked at Sarah. She was beaming and happy.

"That's fantastic. I know how much building the community means to you. It's admirable that you're going to help her. There's no limit to her upside once she gets going," I said, smiling and looking back at Sarah. Dr. Davies nodded and smiled.

"Well, I guess I should get going. I have to get back and finish some reports."

I turned and started to walk out of the hospital room when Sarah said, "Detective, wait! I almost forgot. I have something for you."

I turned and stepped back toward Sarah as she dug through a bag on her bed and pulled out a comic book. It was *Incredible Hulk Vol 1 377,*

*Honey, I Shrunk the Hulk.*

"I talked to a friend who gave me the idea. I put a note inside, and I think there's another note there too."

I looked from the comic book up to Sarah, her smile bright. "Thank you. This is very thoughtful. This is one of my favorite comic books," I said, looking around the room and showing the book to Oli and the others. "Okay, you get feeling better, I said with a nod and turned to walk out the door when Michael stepped forward. We were nose to nose when he stuck out his hand.

So I shook it while the unspoken thoughts were exchanged between us.

"Have a nice day, everyone," I said, slowly turning and stepping out of the room, walking down the hospital hallway, thinking about Sarah giving me a comic book. This particular comic book, in fact. *She's a perceptive young lady with wisdom beyond her years*, I thought.

I got into my car, sat inside, and opened the comic book. There was a small pink Post-it note on the second page from Ginger: "Saunders Ristorante Italiano, 6 p.m.; leave work at work." I smiled, folded the note and put it in my left shirt pocket. I continued thumbing through the rest of the comic book. Bruce Banner was doing a lot of thinking while the Hulk was doing a lot of damage. Then I found the note from Sarah:

**Thank you for saving me, detective. Deep down, I knew you would.**

**Rocky gets it... and even though it's terrifying, I believe his actions are rooted in the very thing that makes you a hero. Just... be you!**

**-Sarah Becker**

# Chapter 25

I'd arrived a few minutes early at Saunders Ristorante Italiano, a restaurant tucked on the northwest edge of town, conveniently close to both of us. I was genuinely looking forward to dinner, especially after the wonderful note Ginger left in that comic book. Turning in my car for maintenance and with my motorcycle still at the house, I'd resorted to a ride-share. I intended to secure a table in the restaurant's more romantic, low-lit area, a small investment to show I cared. The place was packed as I walked in, a warm aroma of garlic and freshly baked bread filling the air. Bullet lights recessed into the ceiling cast a dim glow, creating a shadowy lobby teeming with waiting customers in dresses and business coats.

I navigated to the front of the line and asked for the hostess I knew, Charlotte. A few seconds later, she strode up, a bright smile illuminating her face. "Good evening, Detective. It's great to see you again." She extended her hand, and I shook it. "I couldn't reserve the table you had requested, but I've managed to seat you in the same section."

"Thank you, Charlotte," I said, returning her smile. "I definitely owe you one."

I followed Charlotte up a flight of stairs to an elevated, covered patio, weaving through smaller rooms and the bar area. I handed her a fifty-dollar bill, and she disappeared into the crowd, promising to bring Ginger as soon as she could. I poured a glass of wine for both of us from the chilled bottle.

From my jacket pocket, I pulled out two tiny roses I'd picked up along the way. I placed them on top of a handwritten card and beside her wine glass. Ten minutes later, Ginger approached the table, the bright, crisp fabric of her skirt catching the light as she moved. Her smile didn't demand attention, but it drew it effortlessly, softening the curve of her face, merging with those emerald eyes that stole my breath. Heads turned as she strode past the tables in her wake.

"It's so good to see you, Ginger," I replied, smiling broadly. "I tried to track you down at the basketball game. I was amazed to see you there."

"Your champion, Sarah Becker, invited me," she explained, cocking her head. "She really likes you, Jack. I wasn't sure what to do, but thought, *why not give it a try?*"

"I'm glad you came, and I'm sorry I missed you," I said.

"Trust me, it was me, not you," she snickered, then looked me directly in the eyes, "I'm truly sorry for the way things ended. I think I let my own anxieties get the better of me from time to time."

She took a sip of her wine. "That's smooth. What is it?"

"It's a Cabernet Sauvignon," I replied, mentioning Charlotte's recommendation.

Ginger nodded, "And these flowers... You didn't have to do that."

I winked, raising an eyebrow in a slow nod. "Every opportunity with you means so much to me that I'm willing to try bribery with flowers to keep things going."

She giggled, covering her mouth with her hand. "Oh, Jack, stop it. Bribery won't get you anywhere. How's Cooper?" she asked, smiling. "I haven't seen him in a long time."

"Cooper's been up to no good lately," I said, waggling my index finger. "The other day, he just took my cell phone and ran off with it. I had to chase him all the way downstairs and use food to get it back."

Ginger smiled, cocking her head to the side, saying, "There's probably a lesson in there about your phone."

"Oh yes," I chuckled. "He's a brilliant little troublemaker. And you can't underestimate the wisdom of dogs." I took a sip of wine and paused, looking directly into Ginger's eyes. "Seeing you here tonight is wonderful. I was worried you were just being polite. I haven't felt this nervous in a long time. You are so special to me."

Ginger took another sip of wine and nodded affirmatively.

"Ginger, I want to make sure to give you the space you need if that's what you want."

My words hung in the air.

Ginger smiled and nodded, "This feels right. A chance to talk, without pressure and outside demands."

We nibbled on appetizers and finished the bottle of wine when Ginger suddenly said, "Want to get out of here?"

I grinned, a flash of something wild in my eyes. "I've got a telescope set up in my backyard. Interested in gazing at some stars?" I paused, letting the invitation hang in the air. "It's quite the experience to see planets and stars in person."

She nodded quickly, giggling. "That sounds fun." She ran a finger around the top of her glass. "I remember sitting in your backyard with binoculars, looking at the stars."

"Well, this telescope is quite the upgrade," I said, gesturing toward the door. "I think you'll love it."

I signaled to our waitress for the check. Twenty minutes and a ride-share later, we were on my back porch, surveying Saturn and other sights in the velvety dark sky.

We had a bottle of wine, a Celestron 9-inch telescope, two stools, and a cloudless sky at our disposal.

"The sky is beautiful tonight," I said as I sighted Saturn into the telescope's view. I glanced over at her and noticed she was looking up at the stars.

"There we go, that should do it. The telescope is perfectly aligned." I said with a smile as the telescope's tiny tracking motors buzzed aloud.

She shifted towards me after petting Cooper.

The chilled night air prickled my skin, but the heat from her proximity chased it away. I could feel her breath as she adjusted the telescope. A brush of her shoulder against mine sent a jolt through me. She hesitated, then turned her head, her hair brushing against my cheek. A fleeting touch of her lips on mine, light as a feather, made my heart pound. She grabbed my hand, placing it on her leg, and I gently squeezed.

"Oh my God, Jack, it's so beautiful," she breathed, leaning her body close to mine, as she peered through the eyepiece. "Can you make it bigger?"

"If you're referring to Saturn," I chuckled, "no."

A smile touched her lips as her eyes twinkled in the starlight. She placed her hands on both sides of my face, drawing me in nose to nose, foreheads touching. "OK, I think I've seen enough stars tonight." And then she kissed me deeply.

I reached for her hand, and she wove her fingers into mine. I stood slowly, pulling her with me. I kissed her neck, then her ear. Her skin felt like it was on fire while her perfume drove me further into the moment. I got lost in time kissing her so passionately. She touched my waist, bringing me back to reality. I lifted her into my arms, carrying her through the sliding door, which I slid shut behind us with my foot. I took her to my bedroom, where the scent of her perfume filled my senses, blurring the edges of reality and deepening our connection. A tingle sprinted down my spine as her skin met mine, and time seemed to stop, standing still as the waves of sensation washed across us. Because, as it turns out, the most remarkable discoveries aren't found in the stars, but in the reflected light of another's gaze.

# About the Author

Retired U.S. Army Warrant Officer and cybersecurity specialist, I write stories where logic tangles with technology and motive wins or loses the day. If you like Sherlock-style deduction welded to near-future tech or a dash of spacefaring wonder, you're in the right place. I always wanted to be an astronaut and became an instant, lifelong SF fan after discovering Robert Heinlein's *Space Cadet.* I love hearing from readers, so please send me a message from the Website Web Form or reach out via Email (mamollenkopf@graviscape.net), Or reach out via Facebook or X

**You can connect with me on:**

 https://mamollenkopf.com
 https://x.com/almollenkopf
 https://www.facebook.com/profile.php?id=100095237754678

**Subscribe to my newsletter:**

✉ https://mamollenkopf.com

# Also by M.A. Mollenkopf

Detective **Jack Stewart** faces a case where logic and dark technology collide. As pressure mounts, every choice tests the line between who we are and what we remember.

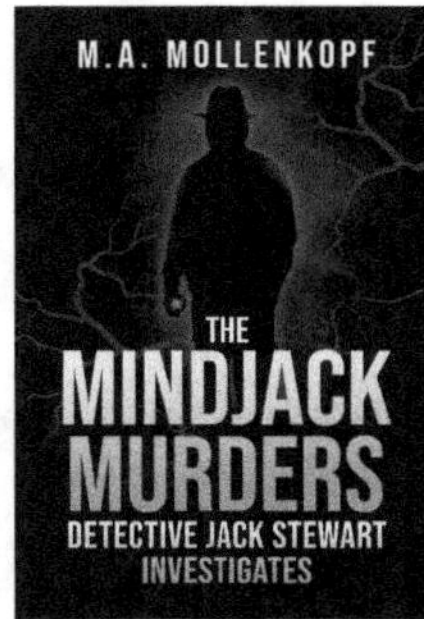

**The Mindjack Murders**

Detective Jack Stewart is thrown into an investigation of a chilling series of murders, all linked to a shadowy faction with possible extraterrestrial origins.  This group, wielding a secret and revolutionary memory transfer device, aims to hijack human bodies and seize power.

As Jack investigates, he fears his own Chief of Police may be involved.  A dubious relationship emerges with the digitized mind of the prime suspect. This tense relationship thrusts Stewart into a vortex of deceit, seduction, and betrayal, challenging him to trust either the machine within the man or the man within the machine.

As Jack grapples with the ethical minefield of this secret technology, he struggles to balance upholding the law, managing intimate relationships and stopping the wave of murders. How can he outsmart a foe who always seems one step ahead?

"The Mindjack Murders is not just a thriller - it's a four-day whirlwind of danger, deceit and dark technology - a gripping tale by one of the most visionary new writers of our time."

**The Graviscape: Unexpected Expedition**
Captain Dave Murray and the crew of the Algonquin disappear from Earth's solar system during a vital Space Colonization Agency mission and find themselves reemerging light years away in a crowded planetary system with no weapons, no supplies and no way to return home.

Through first contact scenarios, the captain and crew discover the Graviscape, the only energy field that traverses all space-time dimensions. When properly modulated, data and even matter can be transported at faster-than-light speeds giving them a potential option to get home.

Captain Murray battles paralyzing personal demons as he works to rebuild the trust of his superiors and his crew while they stumble through harrowing first-contact situations in a desperate effort to get home – to save humanity.

The civilian captain and crew must leverage their new partnerships to try and defeat the enemy's experienced military combat space fleet to save Earth from a devastating attack.

Partnerships are weaponized driving an unusual alignment of allies and enemies where loyalty and love are pitted against hate and uncertainty.

Science fiction fans that like adventure, first contact, battling one's inner monologue and emotional drama will love this epic journey, book #1 in the Graviscape storyline.